'I don't believe in ghosts.' Rebecca said.

'I didn't say I did either. I'm only telling you what happened.'

'Too much imagination.'

'Very possible. But I'm curious about it. I want to find out.'

'I shouldn't think it would be very difficult. There's some pretty ancient people in this village.'

'That's why I asked you. I thought you would know who to ask.'

Other Beaver Books by K.M. Peyton

Fly-By-Night
The Team

K.M. PEYTON

A Pattern of Roses

ILLUSTRATED BY THE AUTHOR

BEAVER BOOKS

A Beaver Book
Published by Arrow Books Limited

20 Vauxhall Bridge Road, London SW1V 2SA

An imprint of Random Century Group

London Melbourne Sydney Auckland
Johannesburg and agencies throughout
the world

First published by Oxford University Press 1972
Sparrow edition 1982
Reprinted 1983
Beaver edition 1990

© K.M. Peyton 1972

Set in Linoterm Bembo

Printed and bound in Great Britain by
Courier International Ltd, Tiptree, Essex

ISBN 0 09 929410 9

To Peter and Ruth, Ben, Louise, David and Matthew

1

'Might find the old hidden treasure – you never know!'

The builder scooped a long arm up the doomed chimney, bringing down an avalanche of dust, soot, and lumps of mortar. He coughed cheerfully through the cloud.

'It's like the pools – these old places – you never know your luck.'

Tim pulled the blankets over his head and groaned. If the man was going to be so drearily chatty all morning, he'd have done better to have got up and gone out. He wasn't really as bad as he had made out to his mother, more fed up than ill, but it paid to keep the convalescence going a bit. There was nothing, really, to get up for, in this God-forsaken new place his parents had gone potty over, so he might as well make the most of his opportunities. Stranded fifty miles from the old familiar haunts of his friends, he had lost his anchor chain: he was adrift. Bed was as good a place as any.

'Bit of a change for you, a spot like this,' the builder said. 'Coming from London, like. Very quiet it'll seem.'

'Mmm.'

If he listened very hard, for five or ten minutes, he might hear a distant cow lowing, or a skylark or two.

'Vicar found it strange at first. He come from London too, you know. A couple of years back. I put a new floor in there. The whole place full of woodworm. 'Is desk

7

fell through. Not that he cared. A very strange man, the Vicar.'

'Oh, cripes,' Timothy thought. He tried to breathe deeply, to make it seem as if he was asleep. The builder got the wrong idea.

He said, 'You're troubled with your chest then? They said as you were poorly when you moved.'

'I've had glandular fever.'

They said it made you feel depressed. But he had been depressed before, if the truth were known. This place just made it worse. Even the eleven O-levels which he had sweated his guts out for the last year hadn't made any difference to the way he felt. All that education, when you didn't know what you were going to use it for, it didn't make sense.

'We'll give you some tablets,' the doctor had said. 'They'll help.'

Tim had flushed them down the lavatory. His father said he could go into the firm with him. Advertising. His father had left school at fourteen and was now managing director. He had got by on his wits. Tim was full of education but he doubted his wits. 'You've done well,' his father said. 'I'll buy you a car for your seventeenth birthday. Then you can knock off your A-levels and go to Oxford and have a ball.'

Tim thought he ought to be happy. But he just wanted to die.

'It's a very debilitating complaint,' said the doctor.

He was debilitated.

'There, what did I tell you!' the builder said. He was half-way up the chimney, scrabbling like a hunt terrier. 'A tin or something . . . there's a ledge . . . ugh!'

He retrieved it, in another shower of dried mortar, and held it out for inspection. It was an oblong tin, like a biscuit tin, with what looked to be a pattern of entwined flowers all over it, much scratched and faded.

'Not very heavy,' said the builder. 'It's not sove-

8

reigns.' He opened it with some difficulty. 'Paper,' he said. 'Old rubbish.' His voice dropped with disappointment. 'Somebody's old scrawlings. Sorry, mate. We're out of luck.'

'Show me,' Tim said.

The builder tossed the tin on the bed.

'Live in hopes. I got five premium bonds and they never done me a mite of good. I never come up for that sort of thing, somehow. There's some people do, some don't.'

Tim heaved himself up on one elbow to examine the find, more interested in paper than sovereigns. He didn't expect much, and was not disappointed.

'Old drawings, by the look of it. Not much good.'

'Nothing the Americans'd like to buy? They buy most of our old junk – Queen Mary, London Bridge, you name it . . .' The builder started hammering, knocking out some of the old bricks to make a bond for the new. The fire-place was obsolete, now the place had had central heating put in, but this little, odd-shaped, sloping-roofed room had been left during the renovations. Tim's mother had thought it would do for a junk-room, and had been astonished when Tim had insisted on having it for his bedroom, instead of the smart new twenty-by-fifteen room that had been designed for him. 'I like the old bit best.' But the old bit, to his parents, the scrap of weatherboard cottage, two up, two down, had merely been a way of getting planning permission to build their own idea of a country house, grafting on to the original an expensive and very desirable wing that had been the talk of the nearest village for the past year. Tim had stubbornly insisted on being housed in the 'junk-hole', and having the walls and the ceiling plain white, not sludge green, periwinkle, or jaffa. His mother had been very annoyed.

'You're perverse and awkward. You're like all young people today. You deride your parents' standards – you make a mockery of everything we've worked hard for –'

'It's called the generation gap,' Tim had informed her.

'If we had nothing – if you *had* to sleep in a hovel, and wear patched jeans and old plimsolls because it was all you had – then you might feel differently about things. It wouldn't be so funny then.'

Tim had agreed – tactlessly, he realized afterwards, for his mother's bad tempers were better pandered to, rather than exacerbated. He seemed to annoy his parents quite often, although he didn't want to. He was all for a quiet life; he was not aggressive by nature, not even very energetic. He wasn't very anything, he often thought, just a vessel into which a lot of money had been poured to educate, to make presentable, to reflect the achievement of his parents. He did not like this thought, but he didn't rebel against it. He would have admired himself more if he had rebelled. Some of his friends at school were splendid rebels. They got into all sorts of trouble, with their parents, the police, and girls. He never had.

The papers were rolled up, yellowing. He pulled them apart and studied them. They were in black crayon, of landscapes, a big old house set in trees, a church, a lake with some cows, a girl. There were a few words scrawled on some of them. On the one of the girl there was the word 'Netty' in very ornate Gothic letters enclosed in a decorated heart, like an old Valentine, and on the most ambitious drawing of the bundle, a rendering of what appeared to be a rambling old mansion, there were initials at the bottom, and a date: 'T.R.I. 17 February, 1910'. Tim stared at this, much intrigued. The initials, T.R.I., were his own: Timothy Reed Ingram. The permutation wasn't very common and the familiarity of the three letters came strangely from this musty-smelling, fragile paper. It was almost a shock. The drawings immediately took on more interest. He spread them out over the bed, rolling them the other way to flatten them. The builder came over, curiosity stronger than his desire to work.

'Hm.' Art criticism wasn't his thing. 'You draw? Know something about it then?'

'Not much.' Tim had got his best O-level result in art, but privately thought the examiners had got the papers mixed up.

'They any good, d'you think?'

Tim didn't answer. The drawings were crude, slightly childish, but they had – Tim tried to think of a word that fitted, and came up with 'conviction'. Although crude, they weren't dull. They looked as if they had mattered quite considerably to their maker, even 'Netty', the worst of the lot as pure drawing went, but strangely hypnotic in her 1910 dress with the saggy sash, and her bold, frontways stare. Tim thought it better than his exam 'life' of Hebblethwaite major in rugger gear, co-erced for the job and scowling with hate and cramp.

'I wonder what they were doing up the chimney?' he said.

'Hiding-place,' said the builder.

'Whose?' Who was T.R.I., in 1910?'

'Chap what lived here, I suppose.'

'Funny place to put drawings.'

'Didn't want anyone to see 'em probably.'

'There wasn't a lot of room for hiding things, the way it used to be,' Tim said, thinking of the two tiny bed-rooms for a whole family. They had larger families then too. There might have been four or five children sharing this bedroom. Tim, who valued privacy more highly than almost anything, had a quick sympathy for T.R.I. who drew and hid his talent up a chimney.

'You don't know what his name was? You've lived here all your life, haven't you?' he asked the builder.

'I wasn't born in 1910, mate. Give me a chance. House was called Inskips. That fits. I think it was called

11

after the people as lived in it way back. My father might know.'

It might have been a girl, Tim supposed. But he thought it male drawing, somehow. It wasn't a girl's flowers and delicacy. It had a roughness, a healthy vigour, that he naturally thought of as male.

'Pity it wasn't pound notes,' the builder said. He pushed his rubble together into a pile against the hearth. 'I'll do this bit of bricklaying after lunch. Leave you in peace for a bit, eh?'

He went out, and Tim lay down again. He could hear the hum of the vacuum cleaner downstairs and the cleaner singing when she switched it off. His mother had gone to the hairdresser's, ten miles away. 'I'll get you a nice bit of fillet steak for lunch,' she had said. He sighed. He put the drawing of 'Netty' on the floor beside the bed and lay looking at it. The proportions were all wrong and the set of the head on the neck anatomically incredible, but Netty was real enough. From sixty years back she gazed at him, provocative, proud – naughty, he would have said. About thirteen or fourteen. Her dress was short and her hair long. Had she posed, like Hebblethwaite major, or had she been drawn secretly in this little room, her creator lying on the floor breathing hard with concentration, conjuring up her image in his mind and struggling to fulfil it with his smudgy soft pencil? The more Tim gazed at the drawing, the more strongly his imagination drew the Inskip boy. He shut his eyes. The boy was about the same age as himself but much smaller, a thin, rather undernourished-looking boy dressed in muddy cord trousers and boots, and a patched jersey. His face was secretive, wary, as if he would hide the secret intelligence that gave life to his drawing. His eyes, when anyone spoke to him, would look down, not wanting to give anything away; he said very little, but outdoors, on his own, he would see everything and talk to a caterpillar basking on a warm path or a robin on a spade. Tim saw him with great clarity, as one sees people in a dream, right to the corn-threshing dust veiling his hair, lodged in the crevices of his ears, and the broken, earthy nails of his drawing hand, hardened by outdoor work. He saw his lips move, and heard him say:

> *'Netty, Netty, Netty,*
> *You are very pretty'*

– making pretty rhyme with Netty, which amused him, for he smiled broadly, revealing a broken front tooth, which he had hit on a cartwheel two years before during a game of tag. Tim knew this, although he had no way of knowing how he knew. The boy was there, drawing, taking no notice of him in the bed, muttering to himself now and then:

> *'Netty, Netty, Netty,*
> *You've got a broken necky.'*

He rubbed out the neck several times, but couldn't get it right. Then there was the sound of footsteps outside the room and the boy darted to his feet like a startled pheasant, bundling the drawing into the open tin that lay on the floor beside him. It was a gaudy, brightly-painted tin with flowers all over it, and 'Marriner's Biscuits' written along the side.

Tim opened his eyes.

'I've got you a beautiful piece of steak, darling, and a tomato salad. Have you had a nice rest? Where's all this paper come from? Really, what a tip! I do hope that builder will finish today.'

His mother put the tray on the bedside table and started gathering up the drawings impatiently. She could not stand anything out of place.

'Be careful with them!' Tim jerked himself up on one

13

elbow. 'They — ' They what? He felt dazed. 'There's a tin . . .'

He had a splitting headache. His mother looked at him with her fussing expression. He wanted to scream.

'Is this the tin? It's filthy. Where did all this come from?'

'Out of the chimney.'

'I'll throw it all away. Sit up, dear. Here's another pillow.'

'No, I want it. Leave it.'

His mother sighed. Tim saw the look come into her eyes that he knew so well – irritated, but trying not to show it. He put the same look into his own eyes. He hated being fussed.

'I'll get up,' he said. 'There's nothing wrong with me now. I'm only being lazy.'

'Eat this first. Then you can get up.'

She put the tray on his knees, and went out. Tim reached over for the tin and examined it very carefully, not bothered about the bits of cobweb that fell into his salad. He wiped the dust off on his pillow-case, and found, very faintly along the side of the tin, a curlicue inscription, 'Marriner's Biscuits'. It made him feel very peculiar. He was sure he hadn't noticed it before, only in his dream. If dream it was . . . but Tim didn't believe in ghosts. Dreams sometimes, could be as vivid as real life, both with places and people. The boy he had dreamed about had no claim to reality. Netty was more real. Who was she? If she was still alive she would be in her seventies. How dull. Tim never could reconcile old people with their past; he could never see the querulous old men drawing their pensions in the post office as gallant young blades going over the top in the Great War. Even his father – now thick round the belly and receding at the hairline – had flown a Spitfire. It was almost impossible to credit. Flying Spitfires had dropped considerably in Tim's estimation.

14

He ate his lunch without enthusiasm and dragged himself out of bed. The boy he had dreamed about was still very strong in his mind, not faded at all, like most dream people. T.R.I. – young Inskip. Tim doubted whether the 'T' stood for Timothy, for Timothy wasn't an Edwardian name. Probably Tom. Tim would have preferred to be Tom. He hated his name. He thought it both effeminate and toffee-nosed.

He pulled on a pair of jeans and a black polo-necked jersey. His mother came up to collect the tray and said brightly, 'It's a lovely day! A bit of this sunshine would do you good, Tim. Perhaps you could walk down to the Vicarage this afternoon and collect the church magazine? The Vicar promised me one – we ought to take an interest in the local community, I think. The Vicar struck me as rather an unusual man, you might like him. Very with-it for a country parson. I was surprised.'

Tim shrunk a little inside. A with-it country parson was the last person he fancied spending his afternoon with. His mother must have sensed this for she said rather more sharply, 'I told him you'd call.'

Tim let out a groan. His mother, with colossal patience, said nothing but left the room with the tray.

Since moving a fortnight ago Tim had seen virtually nothing of his new home ground. Although it was only late September the weather had been cool and wet and unfit for invalids. The doctor had said he couldn't go back to school for some time, and there was some hang-up at school as well – he was going to have to return as a boarder and officially there wasn't going to be room for him until after Christmas. Unofficially Tim was pretty sure that as soon as the doctor gave the word the old Head would have him back at the grindstone like a shot. The school was renowned for its success in getting its pupils into all the best universities, and Tim knew that as one of its current bright hopes he would be subjected to the full treatment the moment he returned. He was not all that keen on hard work so, although he wanted to go back to his friends, he was in no particular hurry. After Christmas would do him nicely, as long as he didn't die of boredom first. Afternoons with the Vicar didn't promise much in this direction.

'Put your coat on,' his mother said.

She fetched his navy-blue midi and he put it on and let himself out into the lane. There was nothing in the lane except their own house, sprawling and acutely new – to Tim's eyes brash, almost an outrage, among the green hedges and elm-trees. His parents had found this delectable site, and destroyed its beauty by putting their house there. 'That's not fair,' Tim said to himself. 'If they hadn't done it, someone else would.' The little, weatherboarded 'Inskips' had been offered quite fairly for sale. Someone else might have made an even worse job of it. Tim remembered it as he had first seen it, half buried in weeds and ivy, swamped by the encroaching hedges. It had strayed in from another century, without even a waterpipe or an electric wire to its name. That was all changed now. The posts carrying the electricity marched firmly up the verge, and some of the trees had been trimmed to make way for the wire. Tim, slouching along with his hands in his pockets, saw Tom Inskip coming the other way, an empty tea-can in one hand, a handful of blackberries in the other. He looked tired but thoroughly content.

Tim blinked. There was no one there. He was daydreaming. It was hotter than he thought, and he felt stupid in his city-slicker's coat. He took it off and hung it on an elm-tree, to collect on the way back. Funny about Tom Inskip. Life must have been pretty different then. The dream boy still had not faded. Tim felt that he really had just passed him in the lane, the face was so vivid in his mind. 'Tim is very imaginative,' his mother was fond of saying. 'A bit ga-ga,' Tim thought.

16

The lane was only used by the farmer and the Vicar himself, for it was a loop that went nowhere except to the farm and the Vicarage. Even the main road was very quiet, for it stopped at the river a mile the other side of the village and there was no way through. Now, as Tim walked on, there was no traffic to be heard apart from a tractor ploughing in the distance. On the right-hand side of the lane the fields were all stubble, on the left cow pasture. A track led away to the farm, and the lane curved to the left towards the village and Tim could see the red brick chimneys of the Vicarage ahead and beyond them the church tower. The Vicarage was surrounded by trees and laurels and very untidy gardens. Tim peered curiously through the hedge until he came to the gate, and then the thought of broaching the Vicar was too much for him and he walked on.

'I'll go and look at the church first, and call on the way back,' he thought. There was an instinct to stay in the sun, after all, not penetrate all that thick shrubbery. The sun would do him more good than the church magazine.

The church was an early, honest, unexceptionable affair set among tall elms full of rooks' nests. Tim looked in, and sniffed the cold mustiness of ancient stone laced with brass polish and damp, and went out into the sun again. 'I'll look at it properly another day,' he thought. It was said to have a good brass in the chancel. But for now, it was the churchyard that attracted and the leaning tombstones, very old, basking in sharp September sunlight, very quiet and still. He hadn't seen anything so quiet for years. Only the rooks, and some blackbirds somewhere in the Vicarage gardens. It made him think, ' "Come into the garden, Maud" ' – it was just that sort of place, unchanged since Tennyson, the top windows of the Vicarage showing through the trees, dark and secret, where Maud would have stood in the dusk. He saw it like a painting in his head. It made him think of Tom Inskip. He would have

17

seen it just the same. It hadn't changed for a hundred years. There were so few places left now; it gave him a strange feeling.

He walked across the churchyard, through long yellowing grass. It tapered down to the compost heap, the elm-trees closing in on it. A few graves humped themselves untidily; it was the cheap end, Tim thought, the stones, roughly etched, all illegible now with lichen and time. There was a rose-bush growing, with strange, smoky-violet flowers dropping faded petals into the grass. The colour smouldered; the roses, the rotting peat round the gardener's heap, a tangle of old man's beard like white mist over the elm hedge. Tim saw it with his O-level artist's eye, and smelt the old summer going and all the years and years that had gone before in the decayed, deserted corner of the churchyard; it all fitted, it was right and his mood was right, standing taking it in, watching a bee heavily moving out of the rose stamens. It was worth even having to call on the Vicar, the sense of ease and content. The colour of the roses was like nothing he had seen before. His mother's hybrid tea-roses, planted in sterile earth out of their plastic bags had displayed trumpeting reds hideous against the new brick. They were called 'Radar' and 'Orange Sensation' and 'Oh La La'. Tim had seen no beauty in them, but this was different. He bent down to take one of the flowers in his hand, and saw the tombstone behind it, askew, catching the sun, and the inscription lined with lichen: 'T.R.I.' Of them all, this one was perfectly legible, as if it had lain in wait all this time on purpose to give him a shock. For it did shock him; he felt his breath catch, was conscious of a quick pain in the heart regions – whether at seeing his own epitaph on the tombstone, or the epitaph of someone he felt he knew quite well, he did not know.

'T.R.I.' He traced the letters out with his finger. Underneath there was a date, but it was harder to read.

Tim used his finger again, digging into the moss and dirt. Something . . . March, 1894 . . . that was the birth-date. Tim knelt down, scowling suddenly with concentration. There was a little dash to signify a life-span – then another date: 18 February, 1910. Tim thought he had got it wrong. He looked at it very closely, bending over, for the stone was small, but there was no doubt about the numbers. The life of T.R.I. had lasted a bare sixteen years. 'No,' Tim thought, 'not even that. He was a month short of his sixteenth birth-day.' Tim shut his eyes and saw again carefully pen-cilled at the bottom of the drawing of the old house the initials and a date: 17 February, 1910. He remembered it perfectly well. He looked at the tombstone again. The day before. It was the day before the date on the tomb-stone. 'It *can't* be,' Tim thought, with a feeling of des-peration. It was as if the sun had gone in. He knelt with his hands on either side of the tombstone, seeing Tom smiling and chanting his silly little rhyme exactly as he had seen him in the dream. But it was as vivid as reality. And Tom walking along the road eating blackberries. Tim felt sick and dizzy. The scent of the slate-purple roses caught him, heavy and fragrant.

'If you want to pray, the church is open, you know,' said a cool female voice behind him. 'We don't lock it.'

'Oh, cripes!' Tim scrambled up, scarlet with embar-rassment. The awful weakness of his stupid illness caught him and he could not take a step, only stand like a moron with everything going round and the sun striking at him through gaps in the elm, and the boy in the dream still grinning, the wheat-dust on his cheek. Tim thought for a moment that he was losing his grip, not only physically but mentally: the sensation of loss and des-pair was so great, about nothing. He felt as if he had been knocked sideways.

'I say, are you all right?'

It was a girl, about his own age. Tim wished he could

fall through the ground into a convenient grave and be grown over with purple roses.

'Yes,' he said stiffly. 'I'm quite all right. I – ' God, it was impossible to explain. He couldn't even start. He said, 'I've come for a church magazine.'

The girl smiled, not very kindly. Sardonically, Tim would have said. He had been thinking he had spots before the eyes, but the spots were now revealing themselves as freckles. She had fantastic freckles. Tim felt better. He straightened up gingerly.

'Do you often go about embracing tombstones?'

'No.'

'Are you sure you're all right?'

'I'm not mental, if that's what you mean.'

'You look ill. Pale.'

That's more than he could say for her, Tim thought. She had the red-head's fair skin, but it was so liberally sprinkled with large freckles that the effect from a few yards off (as if one were looking at a pointillist painting by Seurat) was of a deep gold skin. She had fantastic hair, bright ginger, parted in the middle and springing out on either side in great banks of crimped frizz to her shoulders. If it had lain flat it would probably have reached her waist. He assumed it was natural, for he could not imagine any girl wanting it like that on purpose. It brought another painter to mind – Rossetti. She was straight out of the Pre-Raphaelites, freckles and all. Tim felt again that everything fitted, like when he had thought of 'Come into the garden, Maud.' Perhaps she was Maud. Only she was wearing jeans. He felt better, and stepped off the grave. He had lost his dignity, but was in no danger now of being caught off his guard.

'I was just trying to read the tombstone. The date . . . He didn't live long.'

'A lot of them didn't, then.'

He could see that she was curious, not knowing him, and it pleased him. He felt all right again, only tired. He would get the magazine, but not tell her anything.

'Who is the magazine for?'

Outwitted immediately, Tim's pleasure faded.

'Mrs. Ingram.'

'Oh. The new people at Inskips.' She looked at him reflectively. Her eyes were plain, unflecked brown. Like ginger biscuits, Tim thought. She did nothing at all to make herself more attractive, although she could well have done with it.

'If you come up to the Vicarage I'll get you one,' she said.

She must be the daughter of the with-it vicar, who had come from London two years ago, and fallen through the worm-eaten floorboards. What had she thought of the move? Tim wondered. She was very aloof. Like a ginger cat, he thought. Not giving anything away. He felt slightly nervous of her. She was a cat with ready claws – 'Do you often go about embracing tombstones?' – very amusing. Tim glowered. He followed her through a gate in the wall into the gloom of laurel and yew. A peaty path snaked to the side door of the house and she pushed it open and said, 'Come in.'

There was a row of bells above the door inside, one for each room in the house, the rooms numbered in curly Gothic writing.

'They still ring,' the girl said. 'Only there are no servants to answer them. As you can see.' She threw out an arm to indicate a great rambling, untidy kitchen with dog's paw-marks all over the lino, and a sinkful of washing-up. 'Come through. Don't fall over the vacuum cleaner.'

Tim, used to his mother's impeccable housekeeping, was amazed by the casual shambles of the Vicarage interior. In the hall there were piles of old clothes, as if awaiting a jumble-sale, and two battered prams, and the stairs were covered with stacks of books, with just a narrow way up through the middle. A glance into what was presumably a study showed a desk overflowing with correspondence and literature, more piles of books on the floor and a very old Alsatian asleep on a leather sofa which was ripped all along the front, spewing its stuffing. On the wall over the fire-place was a modern painting of what appeared to be a nude woman, although it was hard to be sure. Tim tried not to show any surprise, although he hadn't expected a setting quite like this.

'I think they were by the telephone,' the girl said, and started hunting rather hopelessly over another stack of paperwork. While she was doing so the telephone rang and she picked up the receiver. 'My mother's out,' she said. 'She's at a committee meeting. Yes, I'll remind her . . . tonight. The Probation Officer . . .' She wrote something down on an envelope and wedged it in the crack of the window sash above the telephone. At the same moment a slovenly-looking young woman in carpet slippers, very pregnant and smoking a cigarette, came down the stairs and said, 'How about a cup of tea? I'm starving for one.' She eyed Tim thoughtfully. 'How about you?'

The ginger-haired girl put the receiver down with a crash and said, 'Go and make one then, and leave him out of it. You can do the washing-up too while you're about it.' Her voice was waspish. She turned deliberately away from the girl and said to Tim, 'Here's your magazine. I'm sorry it's a bit battered. You can go out the front way. It's quicker.'

She held the copy out to him. Her expression was unfriendly, almost angry, as if she wanted him to go quickly, but Tim sensed that he was not the cause of it. Her anger suited her – the adjective 'flaming' would certainly apply, Tim thought, if she ever let herself go. He wasn't sure why she was cross. She did not seem a very cheerful sort of girl. 'That makes two of us,' he thought.

22

She saw him to the door, and he walked home slowly, feeling that the outing had not been uneventful. He was curious about the Vicarage set-up, and he wanted to look at the date on the drawing again, to see if he had got it right. If the T.R.I. of the drawings was the T.R.I. who lay under the purple rose, he had done the elaborate drawing of the old house the day before he died. 'He couldn't have been ill,' Tim thought, 'to draw that. It must have been very quick. An accident. But why do I feel I know him?' he wondered. There was this strange sense of utter conviction. It possessed him completely.

When he got home he found his mother in the kitchen making a cup of tea for the builder. He dropped the magazine on the table. He wanted to ask the builder about the Vicar, but didn't want to in front of his mother. However, his mother obligingly did the work for him.

'What are they like at the Vicarage, Jim?' she asked. 'I've heard they're rather odd. They must be our nearest neighbours, I suppose, and I was hoping we might hit it off with them . . . How many sugars?'

'Two, please. That's it.' He took the cup and Mrs. Ingram offered him a chair at the table, and turned back to pour out two more cups.

Jim said, 'Yes, they *are* odd. Not like the old vicar. He was one of the old school, you know, very genteel sort of thing –' Jim sipped his tea with his little finger cocked up – 'but this one, he's very keen on getting at the young people. He runs discos and he's got a folk-group – they've played in church a few times. The old folk don't like it, of course. That's why he gets talked about. You can't come to a place like this with a lot of new ideas and expect the old ladies to like it. And then he takes people in, tramps and gipsies and layabouts, and he goes to the pub. That's something else they don't like. The other old vicar drank his at home and nobody bothered about that, but a pint of beer in public's another matter. Can't say as it worries me, but there you are.'

'What's his wife like?'

'She wears sandals and a hair-ribbon and works her fingers to the bone – Old People's Club, Women's Institute, all that lot.'

Tim smiled. Definitely not his mother's type. His mother obviously thought so too, for she did not pursue her inquiry any further, but switched it to the children.

'Oh, they're all grown up and left home, except the girl. The one with red hair – Rebecca she's called. She's still at school. The others – I think one's a nurse, nursing lepers in Africa or somewhere, and one runs a children's home, and there's a boy who does something with Oxfam or one of those organizations. You don't see 'em very often.'

'All very worthy,' said Mrs. Ingram.

'Oh yes. You can say that again.'

Tim could see that his mother had already decided that the family was not on her own wave-length. Getting the magazine had just been something to say, to get in, to find out. He flipped through the pages while Jim talked about the fire-place, and found an item on the back page which aroused his interest. It was headed, 'Don't Say Nothing ever Happens!' The follow-up was brisk and to the point:

'The pre-Christmas dance will be at the Vicarage this year – don't be put off! (Only because we can't get the floor of the Church hall mended before the New Year.) Joe Morgan has agreed to do the disco so you know it'll be good. *You* make it good! Any ideas to the Vicar, any time. Kids only – the adults will get their turn later. Book the date now, the Saturday before Christmas. Tickets 40p – proceeds to Oxfam.'

'Poor old Vicar's wife,' Tim thought. 'She'll have to clear some of the junk out of the way before then.'

'What have you done with your coat?' his mother was asking.

'Oh, blast.' Tim remembered hanging it on the tree. He went back down the lane to fetch it, and came back slowly, kicking the first of the fallen leaves.

'Who gave you the magazine?' his mother asked. 'Did you meet the Vicar?'

She was bored stiff already, with no one to see, no one to ask to dinner, no one to play squash with. Why on earth had they moved to this God-forsaken spot? Now the excitement of building the house was finished there was nothing, save going for walks and making jam. His mother had never made jam in her life.

'No, the Vicar's daughter.'

'Rebecca?'

'I suppose so.'

'What's she like?'

'Pretty ghastly. Freckles and a bad temper.'

His mother laughed. She had an attractive, musical laugh which she used a lot in company. Sometimes it made Tim shrink inside. When she used it on his own friends . . . She was very attractive and young-looking, and liked to be friends with his friends, and they thought she was terrific and said things like, 'Not like my old hag of a parent,' but Tim often wished he had an old hag. A homely old hag who had no ambitions for him. He could say, 'I think I'll leave school and get a job on the petrol pumps,' and she'd nod her head and smile and say, 'Why not? Good idea.' He wondered what Rebecca's mother was like with her committee meetings and *sandals* – cripes, she must be just as ghastly in her opposite way. Was he hard to please? He did in fact like quite a lot of his friends' parents. Once his mother had said to him, 'It doesn't seem to occur to you that we find you just as trying to live with as you do us.' She could put him in his place very sharply when she put her mind to it.

He went up to his room to fetch the drawings. Jim was carrying bricks up to fill in the fire-place. Tim sat on the bed and looked at 'Netty' again. Then at the old house. He had been right about the dates. It was the day before. Surely the two T.R.I.s were the same person? It couldn't be a very common permutation in a small village, and the I for a surname was pretty uncommon. He told Jim what had happened. Jim was gratifyingly impressed.

'Well now, that's queer, eh?' He looked over Tim's shoulder and Netty looked back at them from her bold eyes. 'She'd know what happened, I daresay. Whoever she was.'

Who was she? Tim wanted desperately to know. Did the heart and all the loving decorations mean that Tom Inskip had loved Netty? It was easy enough to be in love at sixteen; although it was slightingly called calf-love, there was nothing slight about the pain and the pleasure.

'Did you ask your father about Inskips?' he asked.

'No, he wasn't in.'

'I'd love to know what happened.'

'Well, there's records about things.' Jim started mixing mortar with a trowel, sloshing it down and scooping it up with satisfactory noises. 'Births and deaths. It'd be in the church, wouldn't it?'

'That's a point.'

Back to the Vicarage again. The idea of asking Rebecca did not discourage him. It was a prospect tinged with excitement in fact, like holding one's hand to a wild fox at bay. His curiosity was stronger than his apprehension. He smoothed the drawing out on his lap and looked at it carefully. The more one looked at it the more compelling it became, the more mocking and alive the light in the eye. What if, today, she was just a fat old lady living in a council house? She might be in the village now, getting tea, putting the kettle on. But Tom Inskip had died; did Netty know how? Tim knew that she did. Netty looked at Tim, and the image of the artist grew again in his mind; he saw the boy standing by the

26

fire-place. It should have been Jim, bricklaying, but it was the brown-faced boy with the secretive eyes. He was looking at Tim, grinning. 'Find out,' he said.

'Yes, I will,' Tim said.

'But be careful it doesn't happen to you.'

'What do you mean?'

'Are you all right, mate?'

Tim blinked. The figure by the fire-place was Jim, trowel in hand, looking at him with a good deal of concern.

'Yes,' Tim muttered. He turned away. He wasn't quite sure.

2

'I don't believe in ghosts,' Rebecca said.

'I didn't say I did, either. I'm only telling you what happened.'

'Too much imagination.'

'Very possible. But I'm curious about it. I want to find out.'

'I shouldn't think it would be very difficult. There's some pretty ancient people in this village.'

'That's why I asked you. I thought you would know who to ask.'

'You could start with Holy Moses. He's tying up the dahlias outside the French windows. He comes and does the gardening here. We didn't ask him to, but he likes doing it and it keeps him happy. You couldn't get anyone much older than him. I'll introduce you.'

They knew that Tom Inskip had existed because he was in the church register. Rebecca had obligingly looked him up: Thomas Robert Inskip, born 21st March 1894, baptized 21st April 1894, confirmed 4th July 1906, died 18th February 1910.

In 1910 the village had consisted of the Vicarage and church, the local 'big house' known as Curlews, the pub, the farm, the school, four or five substantial houses, and a couple of dozen cottages including one or two outlying ones like Inskips. It was quite plain to Tim what had existed in 1910; discounting the row of 1930 council houses and the eight modern bungalows, the village in Tom Inskip's day had been small and compact. Tom would probably, like all the other village boys, have worked on the farm. The land-owner had lived at Curlews and his bailiff had lived at the farm. Rebecca knew that much, because Curlews had lately been in the news and its past briefly discussed. Its present owners wanted to sell it to a building firm, and a gravel business was also interested in the grounds, and several planning inquiries were in hand. Rebecca was very scornful of these.

'Sharks,' she said. 'Money, money, money. Even here.'

'Well . . .' Tim, grounded by his parents in business acumen, could see the possibilities.

'Have you seen it? Walked through the grounds?'

'No.'

'It's so beautiful it hurts.' Rebecca had a way of saying unexpected, very personal, things in her brisk, hard voice. Her aloof manner hid a good deal, Tim suspected. It was as if she wanted to make a point of being plain and hard and without charm. It was a sort of armour. Tim could not imagine anyone daring to make a pass at her. She was a hedgehog. 'Trust my luck,' he thought gloomily, following her along the gravel path to the dahlia beds.

Holy Moses was cutting off the dead heads, throwing them in a wheelbarrow. He was a tiny, brown, earth-coloured gnome of a man with a white moustache. Tim looked at him and thought, 'In a minute he might tell me what happened.' And then it would all be over as soon as it began, the tantalizing story behind the dates. But then with this uncanny feeling of certainty that he had experienced before, he knew quite well that it would not. Holy Moses would tell him so much and no more. A crumb. Tom Inskip would still be laughing, Tim knew, before any of them had so much as muttered a word.

He was quite right. Rebecca introduced him and told Holy Moses what he was after, and the old man scratched his head and said, 'Yes, there were a Tom Inskip. He were at the village school, but he were younger'n me. He were still in standard three when I left. I worked on the land for a year or so and then as soon as I could I joined the army. That's all there was for the lads, the farm or the army. So what happened to him, I dunno. He weren't here when I come back.'

'He had an accident?'

'Maybe.'

'You don't know anyone else who might know?'

'Oh, well, we're getting few and far between now, us old 'uns, you know. And them as might remember they're gone away or gone deaf or summat. I'll tell you one thing. I got a photograph of us lot at the school. It were taken the summer afore I left. And young Inskip is on that, I could show you, if you're so set on it.'

'Oh yes! That would be terrific!'

'When I knock off here then, you can come along wi' me and I'll show it you. I can put my hand on it quite easy.'

'Yes.'

'Lunchtime. I knock off about twelve.'

'Very well.'

'Netty might be on it too,' Rebecca said. 'Did you know a girl called Netty, Moses?'

'There were no girl called Netty in the school, no. Not when I were there. There were a Hetty. Hetty Prior. Perhaps you mean her?'

But Tom wouldn't have written Netty if it was Hetty.

'She died of the consumption. I remember that. I remember the old vicar here too – him what was vicar when I were a lad. I used to cut the grass for him, wi' a scythe it were. He weren't like your dad, miss, he were a very fierce man. We was all scared out of our wits when he were about. Brimstone Bellinger we used to call him. We boys didn't like him one bit. Him and the master at Curlews, Mr. Pettigrew as owned all the land, and old Brimstone as owned our souls.'

Old Brimstone, no doubt, had baptized, confirmed, and buried Tom Inskip. Who planted the purple rose? Was it Netty? No, Tim thought, it wasn't Netty. He knew it wasn't Netty, but he didn't know how he knew.

'We'll come back at twelve, then,' Rebecca said. 'And you can show Tim the photograph.'

'Yes, miss. I'll do that. When I'm finished with these dahlias.'

Tim felt a slight consternation at Rebecca's intimation that they were going to spend the next hour and a half together, and wondered what on earth they would find to talk about. She wasn't his sort at all. She made him feel inadequate with her strong, dour personality. He felt positively feeble in her presence. She walked back down the path towards the kitchen door, and he followed in silence.

She said, 'We'll have a coffee, and then I'll show you Curlews. And you can tell me if you think it's a good site for a housing estate.'

'Take that,' Tim thought.

They went into the kitchen, which was a bit tidier than it had been before. The pregnant girl was sitting at the table reading a comic, and Rebecca said to her bluntly, 'Get out.'

'Very nice,' the girl said sarcastically.

'Go on. Beat it.'

Tim looked politely into the middle distance, pretending he wasn't there, and the girl got heavily to her feet.

'You'd like me to stay, wouldn't you?' she said to Tim.

Tim's public-school upbringing rushed a suitable

31

reply to his lips: 'I'm afraid it's not my business.' He was aware of a flinty, amused dart from Rebecca's eyes, and was intensely irritated by the embarrassing situations she kept witnessing him in. He turned away, prepared to go, but Rebecca said sharply, 'Sit down. You want a coffee, don't you? Mary is going.' To emphasize the last fact she put her hand between the girl's shoulder-blades and pushed her firmly towards the door. The girl disappeared, muttering, and Rebecca slammed the door after her.

'Huh.' Rebecca filled the kettle, scowling. 'I'm sorry about that.'

Tim said nothing. He was thinking what a pity it was that Rebecca wasn't a pretty, laughing, flirty little thing like some of the girls at home. Then his convalescence would look altogether brighter. As it was he seemed to have got himself lumbered.

'There's always people in this house,' she said. 'It's horrible. Like living in a hotel. I don't see why I have to be nice to them. Not when they're like her.'

'You mean people your father takes in? Because of his trade?'

'That's one way of putting it, yes. He only takes really genuine cases when there's absolutely nowhere else – she's only for a few days, to be fair – but you get a bit fed up with it. They're often so horrid, you see. It's easy to be Christian when it's nice people that need helping. I'm no good at it.'

Tim remembered Jim's report of the sister that nursed lepers and the brother in Oxfam. They were good at it, obviously. Was she the odd one out? He felt slightly more sympathetic.

'You don't want to do good works for a living?'

She shrugged. 'I'm doing social science. I'm going to be a probation officer. What are you going to do?'

'I'm going into advertising.'

'Is your father in advertising?'

'Yes.'

'That's terrible.'

'It's no worse than your being a probation officer because your father's in the good-works business.'

'Advertising is immoral. All that money – for what?'

She had a down on money, Tim thought. It fitted, he supposed. He wasn't going to be drawn.

'Why aren't you at school today?' He changed the subject.

'Why aren't you?'

'I'm off sick.'

'I just didn't feel like it. My parents are at a con-ference. I won't tell them.'

'You'll lie to them? With your upbringing?'

'No. I won't say anything, and they won't ask.'

'How beautifully simple,' Tim thought. His mother always asked. 'Did you have games today? What have you got for prep? What marks did you get for that essay? How's that boy that fell out of the science lab window? Was Turner really smoking reefers at the summer hop? Is he going to get expelled?'

'How marvellous,' he said, with real envy.

'Is your mother that blonde woman in the Rover two thousand?'

'Yes.' Tim was wary. If she was going to be rude, he could always attack with the sandals and hair-ribbon. But she didn't say anything else, inwardly digesting, pointedly silent. The kettle was steaming and she fetched the instant coffee from the dresser, and got out two mugs.

'My parents,' she said, measuring the coffee care-fully, 'haven't time to notice what I do, or don't do.'

It was a dramatic statement, which Tim's instinct was to shy away from.

'You're pretty lucky then,' he said abruptly. 'It's better than being – ' He paused.

Rebecca said, 'Molly-coddled?' She smiled.

33

Tim was furious but managed not to show it. He said distantly, 'It wasn't the word I was going to use, no.'

'Pressurized? By a high-powered ad-man and an ambitious mama. I hear you've got eleven O-levels. Five more than me. You must be revoltingly swottish.'

Tim could have used the word swot in a different way. She was a wasp with a vicious sting. He withdrew, closing up. It was his natural defence, not to give anything away. Not to show that anything mattered.

She poured out the coffee and said, 'Sugar?'

He shook his head. She pushed the coffee across the table and he took it without thanking her. If her parents had spent as much money on her education as his had on his behalf, he had no doubt she could equal his score. She was sharp enough. Sharp as a needle. A hypodermic.

After a long silence, she said, 'Sorry.' She was looking into her coffee. 'Sour grapes, really. I'm going to have a hard job doing what my parents want.'

'You don't *have* to, do you? What do you want anyway?'

'Oh, keep hens or something.'

The vein of sympathy flicked again. He didn't want to go into advertising either. He wasn't going to tell her this, though.

'It was easier in old Holy Moses' day – the farm or the army,' he said. 'I don't suppose Tom Inskip had much choice.'

'I wonder if he was happy? If there's no choice at all, do you just accept? Does it make you happy?'

'It depends on your temperament. If you're easy, it's fine. But if you're clever and a fighter by nature, you protest. And come up against the Brimstones and the Pettigrews. It must have been very hard to protest.'

'Tom wouldn't have had the time if he died at fifteen.'

'No. It's just as well someone did, though.'

'Else we wouldn't have all these opportunities we

34

don't know how to make use of.' Rebecca's voice was sarcastic.

'Full circle,' Tim said. 'Your wanting to go back to chicken-farming, I mean. I bet the vicar's daughter then would have given her ears for a bit of your freedom.'

'You mean all the time she was feeding the chickens she was thinking up pamphlets for the Votes for Women movement? Well, I'm no protester. I just want a chance to vegetate.'

'You said it was me who was pressurized,' Tim reminded her.

'Yes, well – ' For the first time she was at a loss. Tim suspected that she found her family's selfless ideals too much to live up to. It wasn't pressure of the kind he was subjected to, but possibly, although more subtle, far more difficult to combat. To opt out of that would mean that one just wasn't good enough, using 'good' in its fullest sense, and that was hard to face.

She got up and put the empty coffee cups in the sink.

'Let's go and look at Curlews.' Her voice was abrupt. Prickles out again. Tim, having got the measure of her, felt better prepared, easier in her presence. He thought he could probably give as good as he got. He took his mind off her and gave it back to the reason for his visit. Getting mixed up with Rebecca was incidental to finding out about Tom Inskip, his private ghost. Tom Inskip would have known Curlews, gone there for a job, no doubt, and worked for the boss-man, Mr. Pettigrew. He was dying to see the photograph. Suppose Tom Inskip turned out to be a fat boy with a mean face and sticking-out ears? His dream would die.

They went through the churchyard and out into the road. The pub was opposite, and the few pretty old houses that formed the kernel of the village. There was a widening of the road, with grass verges, and the post office and the general store, then a big house which belonged to the doctor, surrounded by rough woodland.

Between the doctor's house and the general store a foot-path led off away from the road, hard against the wood. The path was firm and dark, of hard-pressed leaves. There was a notice that said 'Footpath to Curlews'.

'The main entrance is farther down the road,' Rebecca said. 'This is a short cut. There's a right of way through the park – you can't go into the gardens of course. It's privately owned now by some London man. He's a property developer, and he must have bought it with an eye to doing something with it, although the story goes that he bought it from old Miss Pettigrew just as a place to retire to. She was very against de-velopers and wouldn't have anything to do with them.'

'Is she still around?' Tim asked. 'She might know.'

'She's dead now. She died soon after she left here. Look, you can see the end of the churchyard through here. Where you were the other day. It backs on to the park. There was a gate through once but it's all grown over now. I think once there must have been a direct way from the church to Curlews, without coming out on to the road.'

'Perhaps when old Pettigrew and Brimstone Bel-linger ran the village. They probably boozed together.'

'Brimstone Bellinger was vicar from 1905 to 1914. There's a brass plate up to him. The Rev. James Augustus St. John Bellinger. Nothing about Brim-stone. I don't know where he went in 1914. He's not buried here.'

'Did he have any children?'

'I don't know. You'll have to ask Moses.'

Tim began to see what Rebecca had meant about the park not being a place for a modern housing estate. The woods fell back from the path and the ground dipped into a long shallow valley with a lake in the bottom. The woods above it on both sides gave it a strange secrecy, the water unruffled by the fresh autumn breeze, dark and deep and still. What did it know? Tim wondered.

What had it seen? He was getting like a detective inspector, rooting out his little mystery. He saw Brimstone Bellinger, stout and bull-brained, striding over to Curlews – no, riding probably . . . already Tim had no affection for Brimstone Bellinger.

'Are there stables at the Vicarage?' he asked Rebecca.

'Yes,' she said.

You could see what might have been the vicar's route, Tim thought, crossing at right-angles to their own. But would he have ridden his horse through the churchyard? Very unseemly. Perhaps he walked after all. Frightening everyone out of their wits, according to Holy Moses. How did that relate to being a Christian minister? How very imperfect life was, that a man whose living was teaching love was a bully. And that, now, this quiet place was threatened with destruction.

'If there weren't, I couldn't have had Fred,' Rebecca said.

What on earth was she talking about? Tim gave her a nervous glance, his own thoughts having dragonflied off-course.

'Fred's a horse,' she said.

'You've got a horse?' He was amazed.

'Yes. A member of the choir saved him from the knacker's at market, so he ended up with us, of course.'

Tim grinned. 'Sanctuary. Your father's trade again?'

'Yes. If they were all as nice as him, though, I'd have no complaints.' She actually smiled. 'You like the place?'

'Yes.'

'You can see the house from here. Through the trees. It's Elizabethan. See – from here . . .'

There *was* a ride, cutting a swathe through the trees. On the brow of the ridge the house could be seen, serene, symmetrical, a warmth of red brick against the trees that hemmed it round. It looked familiar to Tim, but he could not think why. He felt he had stood in this spot before.

'Do you like it?'

'Yes.'

It seemed to matter to her that he should. But he couldn't go on about it. It was a very cut-off, silent place, almost too secret, verging on the sinister. Why did he feel he had been here before? They had continued on along the track and stood by the water's edge, and Rebecca was leaning against a tree, looking at the water. She had kicked off her sandals and was squidging the damp earth between her toes. Tim felt very urban and constricted – and rather tired. He hadn't walked so far since he had been ill. He hoped she would decide to walk back when she had finished being a nature girl.

'There are things, here,' she said, 'flowers, I mean, you don't find very often now. And nightingales. If you come in the evening –'

It wasn't an act, Tim decided. This was her setting. Her face was very serious. This sort of beauty *did* hurt her then. With her hair and her freckles she was dark gold like the bracken on the slope behind her; she fitted. He stared past her into the water of the lake, and saw that it was very clear, and deep; sunlight coming through the trees sent spears into it, gold again, another world, shining above and losing itself below in darkness. Its bed was black and cold and unknowable. Tim wouldn't have swum in it for a hundred pounds. He shrugged, and turned away. He was thinking: a probation officer! She came after him slowly, carrying her sandals, not saying anything. She was so solitary in her way that Tim could say nothing to her either. He felt he could not begin to know her.

By the time they got back to the house he felt pretty bad, boneless and sweating. He would not admit it to her, and knew that he'd have to cover up to his mother when he got home too, so steeled himself to finish the morning as planned. Holy Moses had finished and was cleaning his tools (it had never occurred to Tim that one should clean a spade).

'I'll be right with you,' he said.

Ten minutes later they were following him round the back of his downtrodden little cottage, one of the pretty ones that Tim had noted earlier with Rebecca (but not very comfortable to live in, he now noted). The kitchen smelt dank and mousy. Holy Moses ushered them through into the living-room and urged them to sit down while he started rummaging through the drawers of an ancient sideboard. Tim wondered if this is what the living-room of Inskips had looked like once, so cramped and filled with table. He was glad to sit down; he felt dizzy and ill.

'It were one of them photographers that come round. Everyone goes to school in their clean clothes and the teacher – she lines us up – she used to get so flustered – it were a rare bit of excitement and we was all wriggling about . . . Here we are, just look at us! That's me in the back row, on the end. Here –'

He held the photograph out, leaning over Tim's shoulder to point himself out. Tim took it, and saw it shaking in his hand. Rebecca came across.

'Let's see.'

It was brown and faded, showing about thirty children in three lines, the teacher standing at the side smiling grimly. Tim skimmed the three rows of faces for the one he knew. There was no doubt at all in his mind for whom he was looking, no doubt at all that he would find him.

'There.' He pointed.

Tom was in the middle row, his head down, looking sideways at the boy next to him, obviously trying to compress uncontrollable mirth. He wore a conspicuously white collar, which made him look slightly different from the way Tim had seen him, but the face was un-mistakable.

'No,' Holy Moses said. 'I'm at the back. At the end.

There.'

'Tom Inskip,' Tim said.

'Oh, Tom Inskip. Where d'you say? Let me see.'

Tim pointed again. The old man took the photo and looked at it closely.

'Yes, that's right. That's Tom Inskip. And his friend Arnold Pipe beside him.'

Rebecca looked sharply at Tim.

'How do you know?' she said.

Tim leaned back in the armchair, very tired. 'I don't know how I know. But I do.'

3

Strangely, when the photographer had finished, Tom found that the inclination to giggle finished too. Posing for the photographer had been a lark, but the next of the day's events, the visit of the new vicar, promised no such amusement. Miss Farley was glancing at the church clock, which could be seen in a gap especially cut for the purpose in the row of elms round the churchyard; he was due at three. It was ten to. Arnold was grinning.

'Only two more days! The old windbag won't worry me. He can't stop me leaving.'

Tom scowled furiously. 'I wish I were leaving! Waste of time –'

Arnold, at twelve a year older than Tom, summoned what comfort he could.

'You'll take plenty of time off, if your dad has anything to do with it.'

'Yes. He doesn't see any reason in it – no more than I do. I can read and write. What more do they want?'

Miss Farley, bearing briskly down, answered the question for him. 'The new vicar will want to know if you've read your Bible, I don't doubt. If you reckon you're ready to leave, Tom Inskip, I trust you'll be able to answer any question he might ask you.'

Her fierce eyes raked him. Tom sighed.

'Go inside and compose your brains, boy. You'll need more than your drawings to please Mr. Bellinger.'

The boys sensed that Miss Farley was as nervous of the

41

impending visit as they were themselves. The new vicar's reputation, having preceded him to the village, had been borne out the previous Sunday – his first Sunday in action. The rumours were proved. He was no gentle prelate like the departing Reverend Battersby, but a thundering prophet of doom and hellfire for those who fell from the narrow path. The Rev. Battersby hadn't spoken much of hell. After last Sunday, it loomed horridly in the more active imaginations, one of which was Tom's.

'For God's sake,' he said (meaning it literally). 'He mustn't pick on me!' This to Arnold, as they went through the doorway into the schoolroom. The shadow fell across the July sunshine, bringing its smell of polish and chalk and incipient dry rot, the room unnaturally clean and tidy for the visit, decorated with jars crammed hard with wild flowers, and displays of sewing and drawing (nearly all Tom's) and copperplate verse-writing. Tom, who was bright, could spell and read without stumbling, and he knew all his tables, but the scriptures were hazy in his mind. He knew where there was a bittern nesting, and he could shoe a horse, but not name the twelve apostles without a good deal of groping for the more obscure members. He went to church every Sunday, but he didn't listen. It wouldn't have occurred to him that that much was expected. His father slept behind a pillar. But not last Sunday. 'Too noisy,' was his brief comment on the Rev. Bellinger.

Ever optimistic, Tom thought the new vicar would pass him by for more obviously personable characters to interrogate. Tom never offered an answer, although he generally knew it. Tom was not a worrier. He sat in his desk squinting with half-closed eyes at the thick untidy bunch of buttercups against the window, spilling gold pollen to replace the banished dust, darkened to a curious copper green by the sun behind them. Miss Farley had no paint to offer Tom, but Tom saw colour, although he

42

had no means of copying it. The colour of the buttercups in shade had no name, like the colour of water in a ditch, or the sun through glass, but Tom found pleasure in its contemplation. The vicar arrived while he still considered. Arnold nudged him violently and Tom stumbled to his feet, blinking. Thirty pairs of best boots made a hideous din as they all jerked to attention.

'The Reverend Bellinger, children, and Miss May Bellinger.' Miss Farley's voice was calm and sweet, but there was a glint of venom in her gaze as it swept the class. They were on their mettle; she was putting them on exhibition, like the farm horses at the annual show. They were to do all the right things, and not let her down. Tom felt the sweat bead up under his flannel shirt, his throat go dry. She had a cane in the cupboard that she used like a man; it bit like fire. Hellfire. Tom wriggled inside his hot best clothes, longing for release. His dad was cutting hay now down in the Moonshine fields, and the bittern was silent on her nest where the stream ran under the white-beam below the footpath. God was with the bittern. (No one knew about the nest but Tom, not even Arnold.) Tom didn't believe in hellfire and Mr. Bellinger's brand of religion.

Mr. Bellinger made his heart sink, and Jesus had never meant that.

'Sit down, children.'

He had a voice like a ship's horn. Having studied the thick neck, thick whiskers and belligerent eyebrows in detail the previous Sunday, Tom concentrated his gaze on Miss May who was on view for the first time.

Disappointingly, she was pale and insignificant. She had a crippled, one-short-legged gait which made her waddle like a duck. Tom was sorry for her, because of her father and her lameness, and her task of inspecting village schools in her hot dress with the high collar and tight white cuffs, and the straw hat uncomfortably secured with hatpins. She looked about thirty, although she was in fact twenty-five. While her father talked to Miss Farley – dropping his voice so that the children could not hear what he was saying – Miss Bellinger studied the pupils' work laid out on view. As she lingered over Tom's drawing of a stalk of cow-parsley, Tom's companions sent sneaking glances of suppressed excitement in his direction, which he could feel like vibrations on the back of his flushing neck. The drawings interested her more than the needlework – unless it was merely an excuse to avoid the gaze of thirty pairs of curious eyes. No one whispered or moved, petrified for the vicar, but the atmosphere was full of tension – perhaps for Miss Bellinger as well as for themselves, the victims, Tom thought. Being watched, with her duck's leg . . . He felt a quick compassion, separate from his own self-pity at the situation. No one would marry her, poor Miss May Bellinger, and she was lumbered with her ugly father for life, and playing the harmonium in church, and no babies to cuddle. It was strange, as if she felt his thoughts, for she turned and looked straight at him, away from his cow-parsley, and his eyes met hers. For a moment neither of them looked away. Tom's flush deepened, guilty of his pity for her life. In spite of her plainness her eyes were kind and serene; they did not spear and flash, like Miss Farley's but considered, almost smiled. Tom, his wits scattered by the gaze, dropped his head and fixed his eyes on the initials, T.R.I., that his father had carved in the same desk twenty years before.

'You!' It was the fog-horn, from which his attention had wandered. It had been talking to them for a minute or two, and he had not heard it. Lifting his eyes again, he saw a pair that were neither kind or serene regarding him.

'Yes, it was you I asked!'

Asked *what*? Tom stumbled to his feet, and stood riveted with horror. He could feel Arnold willing the answer to him, in vain. There was a silence like death, the afternoon suspended in time, the dust motes falling softly

44

across the high windows. Miss Farley's lips were set tight, like a seam across her face.

'An absurdly simple question,' grated the Rev. Bellinger. Tom saw his red face and bulbous nose and eyes like the marble chips in his own graveyard, and remembered the inscription over the church door, 'God is Love.' He wondered if the Rev. Bellinger had noticed. He did not feel loved by anyone just at that moment.

'I happened to ask you for the answer,' Bellinger continued. 'Although I know I could have it from the smallest infant here. How many of you little ones know the answer to my question?'

He removed his eyes to the front row and smiled as every hand promptly went up in the air. His eyes returned to Tom and the smile died.

'But I asked you,' he said. His voice was soft and ominous.

There was another silence. Tom could feel himself dropping through the void, wordless and numb, towards the eternal fire he had learned about the Sunday before. He made a painful effort.

'I – I didn't hear the question, sir.'

'Are you deaf?'

'No, sir.'

'How, then, that you did not hear?'

Silence. Not a creak, not a breath. Tom's eyes darted sideways, saw Arnold screwed up in reciprocal agony . . . he lifted them to the blast of Bellinger's gaze, and felt them scutter, panic-stricken, back to his desk. Silence. A petal fell off one of the buttercups.

'Come here.'

Tom moved reluctantly, with an abnormal noise, crashing over the floor. He did not dare lift his eyes again. He came to where he could see Bellinger's feet, and stopped. The feet were very large. Tom waited, blank with misery.

'Look up!'

Tom lifted his eyes as far as the gold watch-chain, and fixed them stubbornly there. Farther he would not go.

'Either you are deaf or you were not listening. Which is it?'

Tom longed with all his heart to say that he was deaf. He imagined saying it, very boldly. He might be, in fact. How did he know he wasn't? He often didn't hear things. How did he know how many things he didn't hear? How did anybody know? There might be thousands of things he didn't hear. Perhaps the things he did hear were only the very loud things. The church clock struck the quarter, and he heard it quite plainly, a bitter disappointment.

'If you sit with the infants in the front row, perhaps it will help your disability, whatever it is. Which of you infants will answer my question?'

A lisping four-year-old reeled off the four gospel writers, and was banished to the back row next to Arnold Pipe, very proud of its achievement, and Tom was invited acidly to take the child's place in the front row. He could not get his knees under the desk and had to sit sideways, so that they all had to push up for him, and there was a huge, muffled amusement through the class at Tom's expense, so that he felt betrayed on all sides. He did not dare look at Miss Farley, aware that she had been pulled to the brink of hellfire along with him, desperately sorry to have caused her such pain. He sat looking at his hands, his feelings all knotted up and sore, and the Rev. Bellinger continued with his inquisition, darting sharp questions at random to a class that was now on pins to please, having seen the penalty for failure. Tom, having been made an example of, was ignored.

The class, well-drilled, returned a fair percentage of right answers, and the afternoon passed away beyond the chiming of two more quarters. Tom, daring to raise his eyes at last, met Miss Bellinger's once more, and saw sympathy in her glance. She followed her father to look once more at the exhibits, pausing over the cow-parsely again. She asked Miss Farley something, and Miss Farley turned round and indicated Tom, and Miss Bellinger nodded and smiled. The vicar's interest was perfunctory. He obviously considered the afternoon's work finished and, after delivering a final harangue about the virtues of hard work and prayer, he gathered up his gloves and stick and bid them all good day. Miss Farley saw him to the door. The children stood to attention, Tom feeling like a scarecrow in the front row.

'Very well.' Miss Farley turned back to the class, the tight lines in her face easing, her manner visibly softening. 'You answered very nicely, I am pleased with you – with one exception.' Her eyes shot to Tom, gangling over his little desk. 'Take down your work, those of you who have it on display, and bring it to my cupboard to put away. Then you may go. Except you, Tom Inskip.'

Tom groaned. The church clock struck four. Five minutes later he was alone in the schoolroom with Miss Farley, the shouts of his dismissed companions receding away down the road beyond the swinging door (he really wasn't deaf at all).

It wasn't Tom's day.

'Good afternoon, Mrs. Ingram – very nice to see you again! And you, Ingram. I'm very pleased to hear you're making good progress.'

Tim felt as if he had been away from school for a year, not merely half a term. He had thought so little about it the last six weeks that it was as if he had come from another planet, seeing afresh the ghastly colour of the Head's carpet and the progressive but meaningless abstract painting above his desk which had replaced a rather nice Van Gogh print of corn and poppies. He had not wanted to come today, but his mother had insisted. She had compelled him to put on his best suit, drive up to London with her, have lunch with his father, go back to his father's office to have a chat with his secretary, and now drive out to his school to discuss his future. Tim did not want a future. Day after day Inskips had grown on him, wrapping him with its eternal lack of incident, its silence, its undemandingness.

'I'm afraid he's getting rather lazy,' his mother was saying, smiling, but sharp and anxious behind the charm. 'He hasn't done a stroke of work all the while he's been away.'

'I don't suppose that will do him any harm,' said the Head, responding to the charm by turning on his own, smiling reassuringly, offering a cigarette. 'A serious ill-ness on top of the pressure of examinations can be very exhausting. Six weeks – a term – off at this stage is nothing to a boy of Tim's calibre. I wouldn't let that worry you.' Unctuous smile. Tim dropped his eyes to the hideous carpet. He felt quite alien to this processing of his future. He wasn't going to join in the smiling. It would have been better if they hadn't visited the advertis-ing agency first. He had forgotten, steeped in the autumn unadventure of his new home, the urgency and pressure of his father's working day, the expensive new offices with windows down to the floor, the incessant con-ferences with and comings-and-goings of sharp young men with superb shirts, long but immaculate hairstyles and quick, glossy wit – he was depressed rather than stimulated by the contact. Before, he had taken it, like school, for granted. But now, out of touch, he had suddenly seen himself, processed by the same sausage-machine that had produced these smooth young gradu-ates, working his highly-trained mind into a tizzy over whether the baked-bean layout had more impact with or without the photo of the shiny-eyed glamour child, or whether the bean tin spoke for itself. Tim had with-drawn, shrivelled, and had not yet recovered. Before, it had never been close enough to hurt, but now they were mapping it out for him.

'Not the art side? His art result was really splendid, but of course of minor importance beside the . . .'

'. . . follow his father in costing the accounts . . . his father worked his way right up through the whole business . . . copy-writing . . . visualizing . . . a course in business studies . . .'

'We are aiming at Oxbridge – do you agree? He is certainly Oxbridge material . . . His main A-level subjects, bearing in mind the ultimate goal, might be . . .'

Appealed to occasionally, Tim nodded and agreed. He was scarcely listening. It seemed to have no bearing on what he thought of as his own life at all. He had to do something; everyone had to do something. What did he want to do? He had no more idea of how to answer that question than fly in the air. He supposed he wanted money, quite a lot of money because he was used to it; he wanted a good car and money to take girls out, and a decent room somewhere, didn't he? Didn't he? Tim felt stifled, the central heating clogging the atmosphere. He saw the newly-ploughed fields at home and the piles of leaves in the lane, remembered the elusive Tom Inskip, whose brief life no one in the village could recall. He too would lead an exemplary life in advertising and leave nothing to be remembered by, save a healthy baked-bean industry. What was the difference? It would be as useful as Tom Inskip's three or four years as a ploughboy or whatever.

'That's settled then,' the Headmaster was saying. Was it? Tim looked up. 'We'll have him back here as a boarder after Christmas. He'll soon get back into the swing again.'

They were both looking at him, smiling. Tim didn't say anything. They waited, but he resisted. He looked at the abstract painting, and thought how absurdly pointless it was. It fitted in.

'Fine then.' The Head gave him a strange look, and got to his feet. They crossed to the door and Tim opened it and went out first. His mother still had plenty to say, and

49

Tim waited in the corridor, gazing out of the window that gave on to gracious expanses of lawn and cricket pitch. While he was waiting, the art master, a quiet, perceptive man known as the Dark Horse, came out of the staff-room two doors down, saw Tim, and came up to him, smiling.

'Why, Ingram! How nice to see you back! I've missed you.'

'I'm only visiting,' Tim said.

'You're better?'

'Yes. I'm supposed to be coming back after Christmas.'

'What are you doing now? In this new home of yours – d'you like it?'

'Yes. I like it. Nothing happens. I don't do anything.'

'D'you think?'

'Yes.'

The Dark Horse glanced round and lowered his voice. 'Your damned results, Ingram – I haven't a hope in hell of getting you into what they consider my useless class except for an odd half-hour here and there. They're all after you for A-levels – Masters, Jackson, Biggs-Smith. When I suggested your taking A-level art they just laughed. Art is only for drop-outs in this school, you know that.'

'Yes, I know.'

'This is what you've been discussing this afternoon – your course?'

'Yes.'

'What's it to be?'

Tim outlined the gist of what he had heard. The Dark Horse groaned and smote his forehead.

'I knew it. Ingram – go home, go on doing nothing, think again. I know this is heresy but, God – I've been in your father's place, I know what it's like. You're not – you're not for that.' He turned away, and stared out across the playing-field. Tim felt as if his brain had turned over in his head.

'This breathing space you've had – still have – use it,' the Dark Horse said. 'It might be the best thing that ever happened to you. Don't quote me, will you? Forget, if you like, but I feel better for having said it.'

Tim nodded.

His mother turned to him, having said her last farewell to the Headmaster.

'Well, Tim? Are we through?'

They departed down the corridor, leaving the Headmaster at the door, the Dark Horse at his elbow. The Headmaster smiled and said, 'Don't worry too much. It'll be five years before he graduates. He'll know what he wants by then.'

'He'll have to fight for it, if it doesn't bear the stamp of parental approval. He might not have the courage.'

'That's up to him, isn't it? It always is, eventually, whatever we do here.'

'It can be hard for them, if we make mistakes.'

'Yes. But life *is* hard, isn't it?' The Headmaster smiled coolly and retreated into his office.

The art master rolled his eyes, remembered the fee that Mrs. Ingram was paying to get her son brain-washed in the desired direction, and went back to the Upper Fourth just in time to prevent the youngest Harrison-Brigham getting his face pushed into the wet modelling clay under the sink.

4

When Tim and his mother got home it was raining hard and prematurely dusk. Mrs. Ingram turned up the central heating and the warmth flowed, soft, enervating, unnatural. Tim stood and watched the big elms shaking in the rain and the water running in infant waterfalls down the lane, thinking of what the Dark Horse had said. The advice was interesting, but hardly constructive. Or was it? Tim sighed.

'I've forgotten to buy a loaf,' his mother was complaining, with a note of near-hysteria in her voice. 'It means going down to the village and waiting for hours for those morons in the general store.' She hated mixing with the villagers, in spite of her new role as country-woman.

Tim gave the matter cool consideration.

'If you let me drive the car, I'll go.'

'Oh, Tim, you know it's – ' But she shrugged and her protest was automatic, meaningless. She threw the car keys down on the table, and some money. 'Do be careful.'

Perhaps, Tim thought, as he drove down the lane, it wasn't really a very sensible risk to take in such a small village where, no doubt, such transgressions by new-comers would be noted with particular avidity. He wouldn't be seventeen until next May, but was fairly confident of passing the test first go. He felt conspicuous, parking the car outside the shop, ducking in through the rain and standing there in his out-of-place city suit, but he was used to the way the locals stared, and looked away when he looked back, and continued to take furtive sideways glances long after he had politely lost interest. In London even Krishna's converts with their shaven heads, saffron draperies and tinkling bells could walk down Oxford Street unremarked. Tim, waiting in the village store, would have liked to watch the effect of such an apparition on his present companions. The shop woman called him sir, which made him curl up inside, and wonder how long it took to belong to such a community.

'Not very long, you'd be surprised. After all, we've only been here two years, and we're more or less in,' Rebecca said. She was outside, mounted on Fred, soaked to the skin but apparently unconcerned. Locks of hair corkscrewed over her cheek-bones, the drops of water spiralling down helter-skelter and dripping on the red, bony hands on the reins.

'What on earth are you dressed up like that for?' she asked.

Tim explained. She eyed the car, but made no comment. 'The mud's pulled a shoe off him,' she said. 'I'll have to take him to the blacksmith tomorrow. Do you want to come?'

Tim nearly said, 'Why should I?' but remembered he had nothing else to do. He didn't know anything as archaic as blacksmiths still existed.

'I only asked because he might know something about your ghostie,' Rebecca said. 'He's lived here for ever and his father before him and all that rubbish. You could ask, anyway.'

'Yes, all right. How, though? Do I ride pillion?'

'Too heavy. Bike would be best. It's four miles. I'll be leaving at nine.'

'All right. But don't wait if I oversleep or something.'

'I wouldn't dream of it,' she said coldly.

Tim, not having meant it rudely, ducked into the car to finish the interview. 'This is where I make a fool of myself,' he thought, realizing that the car would need clever handling to get it out of its berth between a pram and the letter-box and point for home. Rebecca, to get her own back, waited to watch and Tim, concentrating hard, started the engine and cautiously put it in gear. If the Rover leapt forward now with beginner's impetuosity, it would get Fred up the rear. Rebecca, perhaps realizing this, moved farther out into the road, and Tim drove the car hard round, impeccably, missing the letter-box by three inches. Stop and back, hard the other way, very tight and neat. Stop and into first, don't spoil it now . . . oh, so smoothly off! Tim felt a leap of elation, the car's smooth acceleration lifting him, body and spirit. That showed her, waiting to sneer. He put his foot down, the rain sluicing under the tyres, slashing down the windscreen almost faster than the wipers could clear it. Out of sight of Rebecca, he slowed down and turned cautiously into the lane by the Vicarage. The car, cocooning him, took him through the deluge under the baring elms, through the thick banks of mashed yellow leaves, past the sour, tossing elderberry that grew rank in the hedges. Tim remembered it in June, the elderberry creaming with flower and the Electricity Board chopping it back to make way for Inskips' electric wire. In June he had been sweating over examinations, feeling sick; they had come down for a week-end to study progress on the building, and he had been haunted by the Physics paper looming, and the murder of the elderberry in flower.

But the Physics had been passed with distinction and the elderberry had grown back thicker than before. Why did one worry?

But he didn't want to go into the advertising business.

The blacksmith wasn't old enough to have known Tom Inskip, and his father was dead. So much for Rebecca's invitation. Tim suspected gloomily that she had designs on him.

'My uncle, though. He might recall something. He was a stonemason as a young man and he made most of the tombstones around here, so if it's a death you want to know about, he's at the right end, so to speak.'

The blacksmith lifted Fred's foot and pressed the glowing shoe against the hoof. Tim's mind was equally divided between the science of shoeing and the ghost of Tom Inskip. He leaned in the doorway, sniffing the thick, strong smell of the singeing hoof.

'My father shod all Pettigrew's horses, off the farm. The lads used to bring 'em to the forge. He had a forge up the village in those days and the farm work was a full-time job. Me, I moved down here to be near the riding school and the hunters. It's all racing plates for point-to-pointers and Pony Club beasties now.' He plunged the glowing shoe into a bucket of water and the hissing took over the singeing. Tim liked it. He liked the precision of the job and the working of the iron to fit, the satisfaction of the finished hoof, sound and workmanlike beside the undone three.

'I'll do the other hind and the front'll do till next time,' the blacksmith said to Rebecca. 'That water,' he said to Tim, jerking his head towards the bucket. 'Best thing you can drink if you're off-colour. Water the hot shoe's been in. Full of the goodness out of the iron.'

Tim thought for a moment he was joking, and then saw that he wasn't.

'Tim's been ill,' Rebecca said maliciously. Was she daring him?

'They used to drink it,' the blacksmith said. 'Knew what was good for them.'

Tim went over and looked into the bucket, which was moderately clean. He thought of his mother and decided to try it, because she would think it disgusting. It seemed logical to him. They gave you iron pills, after all. He cupped his hands and filled them and drank quite a lot.

'You'll be fit for school next week,' Rebecca said.

He grimaced. He had no desire to go back to school. Leaning against the wall, watching the working of the iron, suited him very well.

'Do you get a lot of work?'

'More than I can cope with. I ought to take a boy on. It gets more and more all the time.'

'Why don't you?' Rebecca asked.

'More trouble than they're worth. You teach 'em, and then they decide they'd rather work in a factory.'

Tim digested this. He wished he were free to try his hand at blacksmithery. Better than a factory by far. The advertising agency was a factory, in a sense. The day outside was gloomy, hung-over with yesterday's rain, and Tim was aware of his invalid state once more, after the cycle ride, and he was depressed. The advertising agency was beginning to haunt him as badly as Tom Inskip. Was he really ill, physically, he wondered, or just sick of the prospect he must face as soon as he got better? He had no way of telling. He shifted his mind back to what he had come about.

'Do you think your uncle might remember 1910?'

'Ask him, lad. He's in the house. Go out round the pigsty and bang on the door.'

Tim did so, and found himself in a kitchen full of cats. He was soon talking about tombstones with a frail ancient man in carpet slippers.

'It was my father as ran the business in nineteen hundred and ten. I was just an apprentice then. But it will be in the books if you want to have a look . . . over there, the bottom drawer of the big dresser. I've still got the books. The dates are on the front.' The old man gestured towards the corner of the room and Tim went to explore. 'I can't say as I remember the name Tom Inskip, but then I don't remember a whole lot of things these days.'

The stonemason, as seemed right for a man in so

exacting a trade, had kept very neat books. There was a page for each job, with the inscription written out in full, and a drawing of the design, and technical notes about the materials, and the price, and 'Paid' written in red, with the date. Some people had a lot written, Tim noticed, unlike the elusive T.R.I. with a mere date. Whole sermons, like:

> *'All you that read as you pass by*
> *As you are now so once was I*
> *As I am now so must you be*
> *Therefore prepare to follow me.'*

Tim sat on the floor, and sorted out the books until he found 1910. February the eighteenth . . . He flipped through the pages, and found that the stone had been supplied on March the twenty-third. It was one of the briefest entries.

'Supplied to Thomas Inskip Esq. of Inskips headstone in granite inscribed T.R.I. 21 March, 1894 – 18 February, 1910.'

The price had been ten pounds.

On the opposite page, in contrast, a very closely-written page described a stone of finest marble: 'To be delivered to the home of Mr. Pettigrew in person and erected on the bottom lawn.'

It commemorated the deaths of:

'Picture	Diamond
Risky	Stately
Sybil	Gayly
Rosemary	Mermaid
Raiment	Rivulet'

who 'Hunted their last fox, 18 February, 1910.' At the bottom, in red, was printed 'Dogs'. The price, thirty-five pounds, was paid on May the twenty-ninth.

Tim read it through three times, then showed it to the

blacksmith's uncle.

'Do you remember anything about this?'

'Fetch my spectacles, boy. On the mantlepiece.'

He didn't, although he read it through carefully twice.

'We used to get dogs, you know. It wasn't un-common. Ten at one go is a bit funny, though, I must admit . . . And a very nice stone . . . Of course, for Mr. Pettigrew, it would be the best, even for dogs. I remember Mr. Pettigrew all right – but later on, after the war it would be . . .'

'What was he like?'

'A bit frightening, as I remember. We was all very careful to please him. He owned all the land and the cottages and it didn't do to fall out with him. He stood for Parliament after the war, I remember, but I don't recall whether he got in or not. I just remember him coming round and giving us all a shilling the day before voting day.'

'Can I copy this down?' Tim asked.

'Whatever you like.'

Tim wrote the inscription in the Addresses part of his diary, thanked the blacksmith's uncle and put the ledgers carefully back in the drawer. The old man had no curiosity and started to talk about growing onions, not wanting to know what Tim was raving about, for which Tim was thankful. The whole thing was a bit barmy really.

'But fascinating,' he said to Rebecca, as they set off for home, bike and horse side by side down the lane. 'The foxhounds died on the same day as Tom, the eighteenth of February. It surely isn't a coincidence!'

'How on earth can ten foxhounds die on the same day?' Rebecca asked, frowning.

'Poison. Or some dreadful accident.'

'Tom was hardly likely to have eaten the same food as a pack of hounds. The accident fits better. But what sort of an accident?'

'A train?'

'There isn't one for miles. At least, there wasn't then. The nearest one came in 1922, because the date is on the wall of the ticket-office. A fire perhaps?'

'And Tom went in to rescue them and the roof fell on him?' Tim braked as the lane dipped, and swerved for a pothole.

'But it gives the impression that they were killed when they were actually hunting,' Rebecca said. 'When it says, "Hunted their last fox" . . .'

'That's what made me say a train,' Tim agreed. 'How else can they get killed out hunting? And besides, Tom wasn't likely to have gone hunting. Only opened gates and touched his forelock and all that. But surely it can't have been a coincidence, them all dying on the same day?'

Rebecca's eyes glinted. 'We *must* find out. Perhaps Tom is a hero, and the whole pack would have been killed but for Tom, who rescued the whole of the other forty or fifty single-handed, and died in the arms of the ever-grateful master, Mr. Pettigrew.'

'He can't have been all that grateful else he would have paid for a marble headstone for Tom too, with a verse and his name in full,' Tim pointed out. He went ahead of Fred, to let a car overtake. 'Besides,' he said, 'Tom wasn't an heroic sort. Not really brave. Just ordinary. If he did anything heroic, it was because he was driven to it for some special reason, which nobody knows.'

'Did they know that *then*?' Rebecca asked the question intuitively.

'No,' Tim said.

Rebecca gave the back of Tim's head a troubled look.

'How do you know?' she asked, remembering that she had asked exactly the same question a few days earlier. She saw Tim's shoulders shrug. He did not reply, cycling ahead, and Rebecca felt what she could only describe as a 'strangeness' touch her, like riding into mist. But there was no mist there. She clumped

Fred with her heels and hurried him after Tim.

Tom would have agreed with Tim's estimation of his courage the day he took Silas and Molly to the blacksmith and Silas got loose in the churchyard. He was a young horse and disliked the whole business of shoeing, so that the ride home had been anything but comfortable with Silas playing up on the halter-end. Tom, turning into the Vicarage lane, was relieved that the journey was nearly over. Perhaps, unconsciously, he relaxed, because when a rabbit jumped up in front of them and Silas plunged for the umpteenth time, the rope ran through Tom's hand and the horse was away, straight over the churchyard railings like Mr. Pettigrew's best hunter.

'God's truth!' Tom felt his very blood turn thin with horror. He slid down from Molly's warm back into the long wet grass and threw himself over the railings in the colt's wake. It was pouring with rain, and the grass was up to his waist, drenching the only part of him – his seat – that wasn't soaked through already. Silas's progress was as definitive as if it had been marked by a forester, the wet earth scored with excited, newly-shod hoofs, not only in the long grass but all across the mown walks between the graves, with a wreath of chrysanthemums scattered and strung out like a paper-chase trail right to the bottom of the plot. There, under the yellowing elms, the horse was cropping hungrily, but watching Tom with a gleam in his eye.

'Good fellow,' Tom crooned, unashamedly telling lies on hallowed ground. 'Come on, my beauty! Up, boy, come up now!'

He approached the horse, holding out his hand, but he knew with God's own certainty that the animal was in no mood to be caught, revelling in the lush grazing and the joy of his release, all his young blood game for a lark and a bit of a gallop.

Tom, trembling, got within three feet, lunged for the dangling halter, and Silas was away with a squeal, straight over Walter Merryweather (1752-1806) and with a crash between the angels guarding Matthew Pike and his wife Annie and two sons. An urn of fading roses went flying and Silas stopped, slithering, on the gravel, and started to eat the wreaths on a new grave at the side of the path. Tom, frantic, ran, and Silas with another squeal ran too, bucking and plunging, all across the soft lawns and with a crashing and a crackling through the fringes of yew and holly.

'Oh, God in heaven!' Tom with visions of the Reverend Bellinger being summoned by the noise, ran blindly in pursuit, sick with fear. The damage was dreadful, the enormous young hoofs freshly armed with cutting iron, the shining strength of the infant Shire mowing and toppling every pathetic monument that stood in his path. The rain poured down in a mockery of unhelpfulness and Tom stood gasping, almost sobbing, his cap lost and the sack that he had been wearing over his shoulders hung up in the holly bushes.

'You devil! You ruddy horse! You *pig*!'

Silas threw up his head and seemed to grin at Tom, his big nostrils rounded in mockery, the glorious strength of his youth shining among all the dim, rain-sodden monuments to the mouldering dead. For a moment, even in his predicament, Tom saw it, felt a stab of joy for the colt who had not yet come to the dogged calm of the seasoned horses through the burden of work. But old Molly, even in the churchyard, would have done no harm; the moment passed, and Tom swore again, and tried to chase Silas out the way he had come, over the railings. But Silas liked the churchyard and trotted on past the railings, round the graves again, throwing up squelching clods in his wake.

Hot tears of resentment at his lot flooded up under Tom's eyelids. Even school was better than this sort of an

61

afternoon, and the trouble he was going to get into when it was all found out was going to be far worse than anything Miss Farley could have mustered. He was petrified that the Rev. Bellinger might appear at any moment, and when he heard the iron gate of the Vicarage garden clang behind him, he came close to becoming a candidate for the graveyard himself through sheer fright. He turned round, shivering.

'Oh, my dear boy! Whatever is going on?'

A woman stood there, holding an umbrella in one hand and her skirts up off the path with the other. Tom, with a rush of relief, and then a succeeding, crushing embarrassment, faced her dumbly. It was Miss May Bellinger.

'For goodness' sake, whatever is that horse doing in here? Catch it at once! My father will be extremely annoyed if – ' She hesitated. ('She is frightened of him too,' Tom thought instantly.) She glanced at Tom nervously, and saw the rub. 'You can't? He looks very spirited.'

'I'm trying, ma'am. He took fright and jumped in over the railings.'

Tom did not wait to converse further, but decided to approach Silas in a crafty circle, pretending he had a titbit. He got close enough for Miss May to start saying, 'Well done!' but Silas saw the trick at the last moment and plunged away once more. Intrigued by Miss May, he cavorted round her, but she shook her umbrella at him and he wheeled back into the holly bushes, bucking as he went. Tom went to head him off and Miss May came with him, her skirts swishing through the wet grass.

'Oh, dear me, dear me!' she muttered as she went, and Tom was filled with desperation, and crashed through the tearing holly. Silas was on the gardener's heap, eating old laurel cuttings. Tom crept at him again, but he wheeled, met Miss May's umbrella and backed in alarm through a row of glass flower vases stacked neatly beside the compost. Tom, spurred by the sound of breaking glass, leapt, caught the halter, and clung grimly. Silas took him back through the holly, whirled him hard against the iron railings of a monument and pulled him off again with a rending of jacket and shirt. A great hoof struck down the front of Tom's leg with agonizing abandon. Opening his mouth to scream, he was pulled off again with such a jerk that instead of screaming he bit his tongue with enough force to take his mind off his leg. Silas then dashed him through a yew tree, was headed off once more by Miss May's umbrella, and pulled up sharp against the chancel buttress. Tom leaned against the wall, speechless and dizzy, but still holding the halter. Silas pulled against it experimentally, but Tom's grip was to the death, and the horse, recognizing it, gave in. A gargoyle from somewhere high above spewed a stream of rainwater over the wilting Tom, and he revived, straightening up cautiously.

'Oh, my poor boy, are you all right?'

Miss May came up, not much less dishevelled than Tom. Her hair, caught by the holly, was adrift and long wet locks of it hung out of the remains of her bun. Her clothes were soaking, the umbrella having been more useful as a weapon than a protection.

'Your poor jacket! And, oh dear, your mouth – what have you done?' Her face was puckered with anxiety.

Tom shook his head, wanting to make a hasty retreat, but his mouth was full of blood from his bitten tongue and he could not speak, and his leg would scarcely hold him. He started to lead Silas towards the lych-gate but his attempt to appear unscathed was not very convincing.

'You can't go on like that,' Miss May said, more sharp now than sympathetic. 'You must come inside and get patched up. What a to-do – most unfortunate! We can put the horse in the stable for now – it's empty because my father has taken the gig over to Meldon. I will see to you, don't worry. You're in no fit state to leave as you are.'

Tom could see that there was no escape, but by the time he had stabled the surprised Silas and caught Molly and tied her to the fence, he wasn't sorry to follow Miss May up the path and into a warm, homely kitchen and to take a chair in front of the fire as directed. In fact it was hard not to sit back and stick his feet out to the blaze and close his eyes as his father often did when he came home. The warmth after the cold rain was impossible to resist.

Miss May, still tut-tutting, had wound her hair briskly back into place and was putting on an apron. When she stood by the fire the wet skirts underneath steamed softly, smelling of ironing and, faintly, of camphor. She made him take off his jacket, which hung very strangely from its rents, and she brought a bowl of warm water and a glass and made him rinse his mouth, and then she brought more water and bathed his leg, which was skinned right up the shin-bone. Curiously, Tom found her matter-of-fact manner comforting; he did not feel awkward in her presence, which surprised him. He felt that it was because she was very true and honest – he *felt* this – she was both spontaneously compassionate and matter-of-fact in a way which appealed to him directly. He did not even feel embarrassed by his broken boots steaming in the hearth and the smelly sock with holes in the toes which she pulled off for him.

'I know your face,' she said to him while she was bathing his leg. 'What's your name?'

'Tom Inskip, ma'am.'

'Ah, I remember. I know you not just because I see you in church, but because you are the boy who did the drawings.'

'You saw them in school last year,' Tom agreed.

'I was very impressed with them. You've left school now?'

'Yes, ma'am. In July.'

'You work for Mr. Pettigrew?'

'Yes, ma'am.'

'Do you still draw?'

'No, ma'am.'

'Don't you want to any more?'

'Sometimes I see things – yes. But I can't draw while I'm working.'

'In the evenings at home . . . ?'

'Oh, they'd laugh. And I've no paper. And the light goes by the time I've eaten supper.'

She did not say anything, squeezing out the cloth. In the gaslight her face was very pale and drawn, the brown eyes seeming to take up a lot of the space. Tom could see that she was quite young, and yet she seemed old. He wondered if her lame duck's leg hurt her; her face had that sort of look about it, a stoicism, a holding-back, a reserve. But the eyes were tender and full of light. He knew that really she was ugly, yet she wasn't ugly now. He liked her.

'What time do you get home?'

He was surprised. 'When it's going dark, now. It depends what's to be done.'

'You ought to draw.' Her voice was soft and intense.

'Why?' He did not understand.

'Whatever talent God blesses you with, you should use.'

A sermon, Tom thought, retracting. He said nothing. He was disappointed in her.

'I wouldn't say it unless I thought it was important. Many people think they have talent when they haven't. But you . . . Why, just because you're a farm boy, why shouldn't you have a chance?'

'A chance for what?' Tom wondered. It was almost as if she spoke to herself.

'Do you like drawing?' she asked.

'I suppose so.' He hadn't thought about it. 'It's nice when it comes out good,' he said.

The house was very quiet, but somewhere beyond the closed doors, perhaps in the parlour, someone was playing the piano. It was 'The Last Rose Of Summer' played with a good deal of stumbling. A talent being nurtured, Tom thought. Less painful to let it lie.

Miss May's next utterance startled him considerably. She had a pot of ointment in her hand and was still seeing to his leg.

'I would give you lessons,' she said, 'if you could find time to come here once or twice a week.'

Tom said nothing, at a loss.

'It would be free,' she said, 'just to help you. Not to waste it, you see – what you can do. You were clever at school. I saw the reports. It's a pity when people are *wasted*.' She said the last word bitterly. 'Would you come?'

Tom hesitated.

She said, 'I will speak to my father about it. And to your father if necessary. I am sure you could spare an hour after work, two evenings a week. I certainly could.' Her voice was brisk, boding no argument, as it had been in the churchyard, then it changed suddenly and she said quietly, 'I am wasted too. I have plenty of time. I would like to do it.'

Tom could not understand her. He was sorry for her. The gentle, underneath side of her that she kept revealing baffled him, worried him. He thought he knew Miss May quite well, as they all did, the lame–duck spinster who played the organ in church and judged the needle-work at the fête; she was, in fact, a bit of a laughing-stock, and at school several of them could mimic her quite well, pushing in her hairpins and limping and nervously frowning. He did not want to be worried by her.

'It's very kind of you,' he said nervously.

'No,' she said abruptly. 'I am not putting myself out to do it. I want to do it.'

Tom did not want to commit himself, and thought he had got away with it as she said no more, but bandaged his leg and passed him his boots and went away and fetched him a jacket that she said was put by for the East London poor. Tom got up to make his escape and she came to the door with him.

'You can manage now? You can get the horses by yourself?'

'Yes, ma'am. Thank you very much.'

'I will arrange for you to come here,' she said. 'I will let you know.'

'Thank you, ma'am.'

Tom didn't know what to make of the offer, and forgot it in the awkward business of getting the still excited Silas back into the lane heading for home. He decided not to say anything of what had happened, either about the damage in the churchyard or the interlude with Miss May – not until questions were asked, at least. Time enough for trouble.

'Well, that's the bottom lawn, and I don't see it,' Tim said.

'Nor do I,' said Rebecca, more disappointed than Tim. Tim felt distinctly uneasy about their trespass around the gardens of Curlews, in spite of the fact that Rebecca swore there was no one in. Mr. and Mrs. Peabright, the present incumbents, had gone to London to buy carpets, and the gardener was planting two thousand tulip bulbs in the beds by the conservatory. 'And if he can see us from there,' Rebecca said, 'he's got eyes that go round corners.'

'If they're buying carpets and planting bulbs,' Tim said, 'they must be planning to stay, not to knock it down and build twenty semis to the acre.'

'Not necessarily,' Rebecca said coolly. 'You can take carpets and tulips with you. If he was planting oaks now, or even rhododendrons . . . yes.'

The bottom lawn was semi-wild, and ran down to meet the trees and undergrowth that grew up the slope from the lake. They had looked for the tombstone in all the likely places, but found no trace of it, and now stood on the bottom boundary, looking back at the tumbled brick walls of the rambling house and its out-buildings on the skyline, and the winter clouds raking the sky above the twisted Tudor chimneys. Tim had this feeling that he had seen it all before, that it was all far more familiar to him than in actual fact it could have been. He had only seen it from this side once before anyway, and then from farther away down by the lake. He turned away and dropped down into crumbling dead bracken, down through young birches and laurel. Rebecca followed, grumbling about something.

'You see, someone did plant rhododendrons once,' she said. 'They weren't in a hurry then.' She was pushing back gnarled branches, her jeans caught up in the brambles. Tim turned round, waiting for her, and saw their mistake in the same moment.

'This *was* the bottom lawn then. Rhododendrons and laurel. The garden must have run right down to the lake. Or nearly.'

'You mean – ?' Rebecca stopped, and looked round keenly. '*This* is where it is? Somewhere in all this wilderness?'

'Yes, I think so. It makes sense, if you think of it. The garden was bigger then. More gardeners – ' Tim was happier now; the scent was keener, the accident a sharper mystery. There was no doubt in his mind that the death of the hounds had to do with Tom, no doubt that somewhere, in this waist-high bracken and tangle of brambles, the thirty-five pound marble tombstone still lurked. His feet were checked and tripped by long-fallen branches, mouldering – he could feel the softness of them, they were almost back to soil, the rotted wood pungent and damp. Did Mrs. Pettigrew in her long dress and picture-hat once walk here with her dog? Mounted side-saddle on her bang-tailed hunter, did she see what happened on

February the eighteenth – screaming through her veil? For the first time in weeks, Tim felt alive and interested, sharply aware of everything around him, from the threads of spiders' trails touching his cheek, hanging from laurel leaves as hard and glossy-green as Victorian leather, to the shadows of emotions long expended, far away in time and crumbled like the dead trees, the last faint breath touching him in this mysterious way, emanating from the places which had seen them in all their first raw energy. Behind him, framed now in the brown fretwork of drying bracken, the faded walls of the old house stood against the coldness of the sky, the colours sharpened by incipient rain. It was very paintable, the way it looked at that moment; it kicked Tim with a desire he had almost forgotten, the excitement just of seeing. 'Oh, I will,' he thought, standing there. 'It is what matters, to make something of that, not of lay-outs for motor-tyres.' He shoved aside the laurel which, devouring the peat of trees and leaves long dead through its wild and greedy roots, the manners of the garden long forgotten, had grown to the size of a Himalayan rhodo-dendron, and remembered the association of laurel with death. To dig a grave beneath a laurel tree was a likely move on the part of the Edwardian squire. Tim pictured it immediately: the gardener in his breeches, muttering at his lot ('*Ten* flaming hounds!') and no overtime. All in the day's work. Tim groped and grovelled under the deep cave of the old branches, pulling aside long suckers of ivy and vicious brier. Something hard. Hard as marble.

'Rebecca!'

She came with difficulty, pulling herself through the tangle with exclamations of impatience.

'You've found it?'

'Yes.'

He could tell she was cross it hadn't been her. They knelt down and rubbed the marble face, but it scarcely needed it – unlike Tom's headstone, lichened over and almost illegible, this was still pure and perfect, its message as clear as the day it was inscribed. Exactly as prescribed in the stonemason's book:

In memory of hounds

'Picture	Diamond
Risky	Stately
Sybil	Gayly
Rosemary	Mermaid
Raiment	Rivulet'

Hunted their last fox, 18 February, 1910.'

'So it was right? Well, we knew that really. But nice to find it.' Rebecca was well satisfied.

'We still don't know any more,' Tim said.

'No. But it will come. It must do.'

'Netty,' Tim said.

'She's seventy–something – eighty, perhaps. Probably in Australia, if she isn't dead.'

'She's still around,' Tim said, sure.

'Who is she then? Netty who?'

'We'll find out.'

Tim's new confidence warmed him. They left the tombstone and scrambled down towards the lake. The water was dappled with flying leaves, their last shred of life, adrift on the uneasy water until they drowned. Tim could smell the bed of drowned leaves, turned to the black ooze of pond bottoms where reeds found root; he had swum, once in a Surrey river, and got among reeds and they had writhed and pulled at him, the current giving them life. He had distrusted water ever since.

'We could climb back into the churchyard over the wall, instead of going back round the road,' Rebecca said. 'We're so filthy, a bit more jungle-bashing won't matter.'

'All right.' Tim didn't feel the slightest bit tired. Rebecca perhaps noticed this for she said, 'When are you going back to school? I think you're lead-swinging.'

'After Christmas, supposed to be,' he said. 'Six weeks.'

'But you're all right.'

'That blacksmith's brew,' Tim said.

Getting into the graveyard was difficult, through nettles and old man's beard and a ditch, grave-deep, filled with deadly nightshade. From the bottom of the ditch, the wall was head-high. Tim would have given Rebecca a bunk up if she had been any other girl, and enjoyed the contact, but she was independent as usual, very careful not to need his help. Luckily for her, she was good at climbing. Tim stood up on the top of the wall, feeling for a hold through the ivy, and she joined him only a second later. Looking back the way they had come, they could see Curlews across the valley, and Tim knew then why it was familiar.

'One of those drawings . . . Tom's drawings. This is it, he drew it from here. The one of the house.'

'The one with "Miss M. says v.g." written on it?'

'Yes.'

'Who was Miss M? A school-teacher?'

'Must have been, of sorts.'

'He sat here, on the wall, I suppose . . .' Rebecca turned round and looked into the churchyard. 'Right beside his tombstone.'

Tim turned round too, and saw the leaning stone and the gnarled rose flinging one last smoky purple flower to the grey sky. It was wintry, magnificent, the colours spent and faded, yet richer in their dying than in their brash spring youth. He jumped down and walked round to the front of the grave and looked at the one rose. It cried out to be painted, not for any romantic associations but purely for the abstract pattern it presented. If you had eyes to see, as the Dark Horse was so fond of pointing out, there were patterns and pictures and excitements everywhere. Tim felt that his eyes had been asleep for some time. The feeling he had had earlier, on the hill-side, stirred him again, that there were things that matter to him very much, and they weren't the things that his parents were mapping out for him. 'What do you do?' he wondered. 'What you're told or what you want?' If the two things coincided, you were lucky.

'I'm going to come and paint here this afternoon,' he said to Rebecca.

They walked slowly up the trodden path through the churchyard towards the gate into the Vicarage garden.

'I don't want to go back to school,' he said.

'No,' Rebecca said, as if there could be no argument.

Even if she understood, Tim was pretty sure no one else would. But it would work itself out. The feeling might even pass, and he would conform as he had always conformed, and become a sharp executive in a flowered shirt.

They went into the house, as Tim had left his coat there, and Rebecca had a Steinbeck book he was going to borrow. It was Saturday, and the Vicar was doing a christening and his wife was at a jumble-sale, so the house was empty – at that moment free of needy lodgers, for which Rebecca had several times expressed her heart-felt gratitude. Tim had got to know Rebecca's parents – they had noticed him and spoken to him in passing, but they never seemed to sit down or stop, and he thought of them as people perpetually in motion, coming in or going out, always on the way to somewhere else. They were both kindly and absent-minded; they never looked worried or hurried, but merely as if their minds were elsewhere, and Tim could not help wondering if they sincerely had so much to do, or whether it had just become a habit to keep going. They would probably be as lost without their committee meetings and welfare work as his own mother was without her coffee mornings and dinner-parties.

Rebecca went to find the book, and he sat down at the kitchen table and looked at *The Times* which was lying

72

there. The Aga gave out a pleasant warmth, and the old-fashioned clock on the wall ticked heavily, comfortingly. From somewhere beyond the hall, down the passage, Tim heard a piano playing. It was not very accomplished, the notes coming unevenly, the fingers unable to find them in time, and sometimes a wrong one discordant, cut off short and corrected. The tune was quite recognizable, though. It was 'The Last Rose of Summer'. When Rebecca came back Tim said, 'I didn't know you played the piano.'

'I don't,' she said.

'Who is, then?'

Rebecca looked at him oddly. 'No one.'

' "The Last Rose of Summer",' Tim said.

He got up, pushing back the chair. 'No, it's not you. I can still hear it.'

'You're raving,' Rebecca said.

Tim went into the passage, drawn by curiosity and a strange excitement. He crossed the hall and opened the door of the big living-room. The room was large and rarely used, furnished in a disjointed, jumble-sale fashion, and in the far alcove, sideways on to the big bay window that overlooked the lawn, there was a piano. The lid was down, and there was no one there. The room was quite silent, not even a clock. Tim stood in the doorway, looking.

'You're a bit touched,' Rebecca said. 'Brain disease.'

'No,' Tim said.

There was nothing else to say, nothing to explain. He followed Rebecca back to the kitchen, took the book and his coat and went home.

5

Tim had the old drawings spread out on the floor of his bedroom. Beside them there were several fresh sheets of paper with his own efforts on them, three shots at the rose-bush on the grave, one of which was moderately successful, and two of Curlews from the churchyard wall. It was interesting to compare Tom's drawing of Curlews with his. There had been ivy on it then, which made it far more difficult for Tom, the house formless and dark against dark trees; the trees had mostly been smaller but there was a huge cedar-tree in Tom's drawing that was no longer there. Tom had put nettles and bracken in the foreground, one frond of bracken sticking up boldly, very close to the eye, and on it a spider drawn in minute detail, every tiny hair on its legs, the mottled pattern within its bulbous outline drawn with loving care.

Tim could see Tom sitting on the wall to draw Curlews, as a lesson in perspective and landscape composition in schoolbook manner, and getting sidetracked by the spider, so that there was more drawing in the spider than all the rest of the work put together.

Tim liked Tom. He liked the spider. Tom drew life with love and spirit; when it was just houses and flowers it was dogged and competent, but without excitement. But obviously Miss M., in proper Victorian fashion, thought that drawing *things* was basic art training, good and wholesome like bread and butter before jelly, and

74

Tom was bent to draw things: flowers and vases and barns and trees. Tim thought that Tom would probably have got on a lot better with the Dark Horse than Miss M.

He shuffled through Tom's drawings again, looking at them more closely. Of the life drawings, Netty was outstanding. The dog at her feet, although disjointed in rather the same way as Netty, was very alive, sitting planted in puppy-like fashion, great big paws spread well out. Tim noticed, for the first time, that the dog appeared to be a foxhound.

'A clue, my dear Watson,' he murmured. There was another dog among the drawings, that he remembered, and something written which was so smudged that he hadn't bothered to try to decipher it. He turned them over hastily, cursing as they still tried to roll themselves up, and found the one of the dog. It wasn't as good a drawing as some of the others, the legs being distinctly peculiar and the whole animal having a horselike stance, but it did certainly look more like a foxhound than any other species. It had been lying face on to a drawing of a tree in very black pencil and was so badly smudged that it was a drawing he had rather discounted earlier, but on close examination it did appear to have something written at the bottom.

'Ah ha,' Tim murmured, excited enough to bestir himself to find an old magnifying glass he had in the bottom of his junk drawer. He lay on the floor, peering eagerly. It was the dog's name, and the date 1909, but the name was very hard to make out. It started with an M.

'It must be . . . No, why should it? M . . .' It was indecipherable, but it started with M and was the right length to be 'Mermaid'. Suppose it was Mermaid, one of the hounds on the tombstone?

'So what? Where does that get us?' Tim wondered. Where did Netty come into it?

He let go of the drawings and they rolled themselves

up, as if to hide the secrets they held. Tim sighed. He turned to his own paintings, and propped them up and narrowed his eyes at them, trying to see if they looked better than he knew they were. They were just good enough to make him want to go and try again, bad enough to exasperate him. The great discontent seized him again, about what life was all about. He lay on the bed and hung over the side on his back, looking at his work upside down. It improved it.

'What on earth . . .?' His mother had arrived. Tim resented her coming into his room without asking and sat up crossly.

'I'm glad to see you're working again, instead of just mooching around,' she said briskly. She looked at his paintings and pointed her toe at the best one of the rose on the grave.

'That would make a lovely cosmetic advert.'

Tim was so angry that he snorted out loud, half-choking. Whatever little merit the painting might have had, it was now blasted stone-dead. He wished his mother could drop dead. He glowered at her.

'You're so much better now!' She smiled at him keenly. 'We might even get you back to school before Christmas if Doctor Pearce agrees. I'll give him a ring and see if he can see you next week.'

'I'm not going,' Tim said.

'I *beg* your pardon!'

Tim, as amazed at what he had said as his mother, but glad, repeated the remark. His mother's eyes narrowed and she stared at him as he had stared a moment before at his painting.

'What exactly do you mean by that?'

'I mean that I just don't want to go. Not yet. Not ever really. Not just to swat and go into Dad's place, anyway.'

'Oh, you're still run down. We can't expect you to feel very keen at the moment. But when you get back you'll think differently about things. You'll want to keep up with your friends, go on to University with them . . .'

'No.'

'Are you serious?'

'I don't see the point. I don't want to go into advertising.'

'*Now* you tell us!'

'You never asked.'

'It's such a big field – you can't reject it outright! I think
you'll feel differently when you're back at school. You've
lost the thread, buried out here with no company and
nothing to do – I feel at a loss myself. I don't know if
country life suits us.'

Tim thought he'd just found the thread, whatever it
was, rather than lost it, but did not say so. He merely
said, frowning, 'I like country life. I like it here.'

'It's not that girl, Rebecca, is it? She's not the reason
you don't want to go back?'

'No, it isn't!' Tim was furious.

'She's such an odd-looking girl – and her clothes! She
wants someone to take her in hand, with that freakish hair.
She could be very attractive, with the right treatment.'

'Oh, cripes!' Tim sat up, intense irritation kicking him
into action. 'She's all right as she is!'

'You *are* interested!'

Tim got up and went out, slamming the door so hard
that some plaster fell out of the ceiling. In sixty seconds
flat his mother had bulldozed him, extinguishing utterly
any faint pearls of light he had been harbouring on life,
art, and girls. Tim made for the Vicarage without noticing it, like a fox to his lair. Just outside the gate he met
Rebecca, coming his way, looking freakish, he noticed,
her frizzed hair like a great cloud around the golden,
freckle-cast face. Just for a moment, her burnished colour
against the coldness of the day made her look quite
beautiful. The clothes that his mother so deplored,
patched blue jeans, a drooping khaki U.S. army parka
covered in mud, and underneath a purple sweater several

times too large, looked perfectly right to Tim. But it was as a friend he desired her, not as a girl-friend. He hated his mother.

'What's up?' she said, sensing.

'Oh . . . mothers . . . life . . .' He felt bleak and useless, even with Rebecca.

'Don't bother,' she said. 'It'll come out all right. It must do. There's something I've discovered. I was coming to tell you. Come and see what I've found.'

If he hadn't been so self-involved, he would have noticed earlier that her glow was that of excitement, not merely freckles. She wasn't going to give him any sympathy, merely distraction. If it was good enough, it would do, no doubt.

'The piano,' she said, as they went into the house. 'It was here when we came, you know. It must have been here for donkey's years. I've been having a root round.'

'What have you found?'

'Netty.'

'What do you mean?'

'I'll show you.'

They went into the big gaunt living-room which was cold as a tomb. Rebecca crossed over to the piano and reached up for some sheets of music that lay on the top. They were very old and falling to bits, covered in dust.

'They were *inside* it,' she said. 'Inside the lid at the top. I tried to play it, and it wouldn't work, and that's why, because they were bunging up the keys. I think they must have fallen down behind the piano once – that's why they're so dirty, and someone fished them out and just shoved them inside out of the way. But look – look at the front – what's written –'

She held them out for him to see, and written in faded brown ink on the top corner of the top copy was 'Netty Bellinger.' Rebecca pulled out another from underneath, and on that was written, in a smaller and neater hand, 'May Bellinger'.

78

'Bellinger!' Tim said. 'She was a Bellinger!'

'Sisters, I've decided. May must be Miss M, who taught Tom drawing. Could be, anyway. Older. And Netty the younger one, who Tom drew. It fits doesn't it? The vicar's daughter teaching him, a sort of governess type.'

'What's the music?'

He knew, before Rebecca told him. ' "The Last Rose of Summer." That's what I heard.'

'You thought you heard it,' Rebecca said.

'I did.'

'I've been thinking about that,' Rebecca said slowly. 'I don't believe in ghosts, after all. Do you?'

'I didn't once.'

'It was in your mind, I think. The last rose of summer – you'd been looking at that bush on the grave and there was one rose, in September. You were very impressed by it, because you wanted to draw it. It was in your mind already, the name of the music.'

'Hm.' It was a clever explanation, but Tim knew he had heard the music. He could not tell Rebecca. He would keep it to himself. Something in him was on the same wave-length as something that had happened before. He kept brushing against it, just occasionally, when the moon was in the right quarter or the stars were just so – he was quite content that it should happen, the ghosts being entirely friendly so far, even happy, if Tom was anything to go by. And if Rebecca's explanation was right, so what? She could believe her way, he could believe his. He didn't *dis*believe anything.

Rebecca said, 'But now we know that Netty was a Bellinger, we might be able to trace her. At least we know who we're looking for. And if we find her, she'll tell us what happened.'

'She might,' Tim said.

'We might not find her.'

'No.' Tim took the music and looked at the piece with

May Bellinger written on the top. It was called 'To a Wild Rose' by Edward MacDowell. He thought of the rose on the grave.

'It's all roses,' he said.

'Yes. I noticed. Is it just coincidence?'

'Part of the pattern.'

Rebecca looked sceptical. 'I don't see any pattern. It's just a sort of mess with a few loose ends hanging out which you follow and get nowhere.'

'You don't see the pattern at the time. It's only later, when it's all finished, that you see that there was a pattern. A logic.'

'Hm.' Rebecca did not sound convinced.

Tim said, 'I don't believe much in coincidence.'

'But everything is coincidence. You are talking to me now only because my father got this living because the man it was offered to got killed in a car accident a week before he was supposed to come here . . . And you're here just because that bit of a cottage appealed to your parents more than all the thousands of others they probably looked at. If the other vicar hadn't been killed and your mother had preferred somewhere else we wouldn't even have met.'

'Pattern.'

'Whim,' said Rebecca gloomily. 'I can't take "The Last Rose of Summer". Only if you're psychic.'

'Why do you have to have everything explained?'

'Because I'm training to be a keeper of casebooks and dossiers and memos and records. It can't be done by intuition.'

'You've got the wrong temperament for a ghost hunt.'

'Yes. But I've done all the work so far. Finding Netty, and taking you to the blacksmith who got you to the tombstone books which found us the grave.'

'You're quite right. I'm sorry. What do we do now?'

'Trace Netty Bellinger, bearing in mind she's probably got married and has another name. Might not, though –

she's the vintage whose men all got killed in the war. Telephone directory, electoral roll. Somerset House . . . she ought to turn up if we persevere. Perhaps through the church – her father . . .'

Perhaps she *would* make a good probation officer after all, Tim thought.

May Bellinger opened the door of the sitting-room and said to Tom, 'Come inside. I want you to draw the fern, and the pot is too heavy to lift into the study. Take no notice of Netty. She can get on with her work and you can get on with yours. Did you sharpen your pencil? You'll want a fine point.'

'Yes, miss.'

'Sit here, with your back to the piano.'

Tom did as he was told.

'Rest your board here, for the light – that's it.' She turned the heavy brass urn that stood on the table, so that a daunting plethora of cascading maidenhair stood in the brightest pool of light from the gas chandelier – a million leaves to draw, Tom thought, with plunging spirits, a hundred million tiny leaf spores, a hundred million veins and indentations and spiderlike fronds, a million million hairs like fur covering the hairlike stems. He shut his lips tightly to repress a groan.

'And the urn as well,' Miss May said. 'The whole group – container and fern.'

The urn was chased with a scene of deer-hunting, deeply modelled and decorated with swags of vine leaves. Tom stared at his white paper and the pathetic inadequacy of his sharpened point.

'Please – '

'Start away. Don't waste time. I'll come back in half an hour. I have to see old Miss Sharp – she's waiting in the study. I'm sorry I can't give you more attention this evening. Get on, Netty. There's no need for you to be distracted at all. Your scales are quite dreadful – don't waste time.'

She stood over Tom, so near that he could smell the faint camphor and lavender scent of her stiff black silk skirt, and watched him make the first tentative stroke of his pencil. She was in her sharp mood, which Tom did not like. He looked at her nervously and saw her eyes deeply shadowed by the gaslight, her cheekbones standing out, shining, the smooth line of her neck cut off abruptly by the stiffened lace collar of her blouse, a gold brooch like a sudden flame in the folds as she turned away. He saw her as an object to draw, like the fern, only so much more desirable, with a lovely form and texture and colour under the lamp. His eyes went back to the fern and he had to stifle a groan. Miss May swooped down behind him with a rustle of her skirts and her sharp voice changed.

'My darling Ferdy! Do you want to stay and join the lessons then, my darling boy?' A large, golden–coated cat allowed itself to be swept off the sofa and into her arms with a contented, engine-like purring. Another sideways glance from Tom showed him the cat looking down at him from her embrace, all tawny-gold against the cream lace, and Miss May's face glowing with the fantastic love she lavished on this indulged, spiteful animal. It was another cameo in his mind, beyond his abilities to put into tangible form, but again desirable, stimulating, full of meaning – unlike the relentless fern.

The cat jumped down on to the silk sofa cushions and settled itself with its traction purr against the hissing of the gas, and Miss May left the room with a last brisk injunction to work hard. Tom stared at the fern, and listened to Netty's scales blundering up the keys behind him. His mind was anywhere but on the fern. After a day's work, twelve hours save for lunch under the hedge in a bitterly cold November wind, the unfamiliar graciousness of the Vicarage parlour – the big fire flickering lazily beyond the brass fender, the heavy velvet curtains close and warm against the spattering of the rain, the soft fragrance of the watered peat from the fern – was too overwhelming to make him feel much like work. Besides which, Netty's presence was hard to ignore, not only because of the noise which she was making on the piano, but because she had a very positive presence that was all her own. Tom had had very little opportunity to speak to her on his visits to the Vicarage, but he had been aware of her out of all proportion to the number of times he had set eyes on her. Her presence was a tangible warmth in the dour atmosphere of the house; she was all spirit and bubbling energy; she shouted and sang and laughed and even the Rev. Bellinger himself could not restrain her.

'This is my cousin Netty,' Miss May had introduced him the second time he had visited the Vicarage. 'She has come to stay here while her parents are in India.'

From the formality of the introduction Tom recognized that there was no intimation that they should become friends. Netty had to be explained. That was all. She rarely came into the study where Tom usually took his lessons, and Tom knew very little about her, except that she was as lavishly endowed with feminine charm as Miss May lacked it. He could feel it whenever she came near; she was like a spring daffodil to Miss May's dark laurel. Tom, at fourteen years old, was far from immune from feminine charm, having once discovered it. No village girl had ever moved him to a second glance, but Netty, whether because she was 'different', in that she moved in another world which Tom had never expected to see into, or whether purely through her personality, attracted him in a way that he found disturbing.

He frowned at his fern, the execrable scales impinging heavily on his concentration. Physically very tired, and with the strong distraction of Netty's presence overriding his attention to his work, he could not help wishing he were safely, undemandingly at home. He could not draw the fern with Netty there – he could not draw it very well without her there. Miss May would be grieved and he would feel unworthy. The evening's pattern was already laid out. He watched his grey pencil chase the outline of a fidgety frond. It went unwillingly, its line a snail's trail of unimagination. Tom's eyes slid sideways, and saw Miss May's Ferdinand watching him from its silk bed, its back arched against the sofa arm with a sinuous, feline ease, a line as strong and lovely as the fern's shape was fussy and dull. Tom's pencil moved, digressing. *There* was something for the pencil to take, to enlarge upon, to explore, to enjoy! The fur and the silk, the great amber eyes with black lines round them . . . The cat watched Tom, still purring. Netty had stopped playing the piano, and there was a silence behind Tom's back which he could feel. He felt as if Ferdinand and Netty between them had caught him. He went on drawing, nervous now – nervous of stopping and seeing what Netty was up to. The cat was so splendid – it took a nature as strong as Netty's to distract him. He was distracted, and felt a bead of sweat gather on his lip, but the pencil had found the sweep of the bushy tail. He worked on. The cat stared at him. Netty hit a chord suddenly which made Tom jump, and the tail on the paper twitched, the line flying off. Tom reached for his rubber.

'You're supposed to be doing the fern,' Netty said severely.

She had turned round and was watching. Tom knew she had, but didn't look up.

'You're supposed to be playing the piano.'

'Yes.' Quite amicably. Still silence, so Tom felt no compunction to go back to the fern. The cat was coming out well. Netty got up and he could feel her standing behind him. He stopped drawing. He couldn't, with her watching.

'Go on,' she said. 'It's nice.'

'I can't with you there.'

'Why not?'

He didn't know. He didn't say anything. She moved away and leaned over the sofa, but Ferdinand got up then and moved towards her, so it was spoiled. Tom sighed. Netty laughed. Tom allowed himself to look at her then. She didn't look the slightest bit guilty.

'Doesn't Miss May get cross with you if you stop playing?' he asked.

'Yes, but it doesn't matter. I get tired of lessons. Don't you?'

'Not of drawing. Only this fern – it isn't very exciting. I don't do any other lessons.'

'What do you do?'

'I work on the farm.'

'Doing what?'

How nosey she was! 'Whatever comes up.' That day he had carted twenty loads of muck. Sitting there now he was very conscious of the fact that, in spite of having washed extra carefully, even his hair, and wearing his Sunday clothes, she might be able to smell him. His hands on the white paper were like knobbly brown potatoes beside the delicate fingers she had buried in Ferdy's coat. They held a muckrake more comfortably than a pencil, when all was said and done; his shoulders ached to the day's work, and he felt absurdly out of place beside Netty, presuming to draw a fern in a pot. He coloured up at the sudden thought and wondered why on earth Miss May wanted to make such a monkey out of him. He dropped his board on the sofa, scowling.

But Netty said, all sweetness, 'You draw ever so well. That's marvellous of Ferdy.'

'You made him move,' Tom growled.

'Oh, well, it was finished. Why do you come here for lessons?'

'Miss May asked me to.' His mother had been very keen for him to come, but his father had the same attitude towards it as he had just experienced in that moment. His

85

father had muttered, but his mother had said, with un-accustomed vehemence, 'Not many chances will ever come his way! Why deny him this? God in heaven, do you want nothing better for your children than – ' At which point his father had threatened to knock her under the table if she didn't hold her tongue. Tom didn't tell Netty this.

'Miss May must like giving people lessons. She's always giving me lessons,' Netty said, regretfully.

'Don't you go to school?'

'No. She teaches me, and Uncle Jim gives me Scripture lessons and Latin and mathematics.'

Tom had to adjust his ideas to the Reverend Bellinger being mild-sounding Uncle Jim to this girl. He studiously avoided the vicar and had only had the misfortune to meet him twice in the passage since coming to the Vicarage. Sunday was enough, in church. He looked at Netty. Bound by mutual regret at this over-emphasis on learning, they smiled. Netty was gorgeous, Tom thought, with a sudden smite in his heart-region – just in her looks, of course – her mind was nosy and addled as one must expect in her sex – but her deep blue eyes were like violets (Tom's similes were bound by a very limited reading-matter – his mother's weekly paper) and her lips like cherries. No – his observant eye rejected the last – her lips were nothing like cherries; they were too soft and mocking – she seemed to laugh at everything, even him; she had a mass of curling red-gold hair that was like nothing he could think of to use as a simile. It was the most beautiful hair he had ever seen. It wasn't like any-thing else at all. Tom felt himself blushing.

It was at this moment that May came back into the room. She had had a hard time with Miss Sharp, who wanted her to go and see Mr. Pettigrew about her cottage which was disintegrating with damp, and she was in considerable pain from her leg, which she had broken as a child and which always played up when the weather was damp, so that she was in no mood for indulgence. She came in at the door, and, in the pool of light beneath the chandelier, she saw the two faces regarding each other with what she could only describe as a glow of such warmth and understanding – was it just the lamplight, and the fact that they were laughing at what had no doubt been a silly joke, or was it her own mind coloured by familiar idiotic calendar pictures entitled 'Innocence' or 'First Love'? – that she felt an almost physical pain go through her of a jealousy she did not think herself capable of. Not jealousy of any one person, but pure envy of a situation so carefree and so happy. They were untouched, both of them, by any hint of seriousness, of responsi-bility, pain, disappointment, boredom, frustration, even doubt, which it seemed to May filled her own whole life, that the spasm that seized her frightened her with its unexpected violence. She felt quite faint at her own emotion, and leaned against the door-frame, her eyes glittering.

'How dare you! As soon as my back is turned!' She wanted to weep, seeing their faces change, feeling the unfairness of it, knowing that it was her own bitterness she was hating. Netty was a little madam; she giggled, springing back to the piano, but Tom withdrew as if she had slapped him. May was desperately sorry but could do nothing to change the situation. It was only a small thing, brought about by her feeling tired and over-wrought, but Tom deserved nothing but encouragement and affection. May had only asked him to come because there was something about his nature, his transparent honesty and willingness, that appealed to her. She was not in the habit of asking all the village children into her home. And since she had come to know him better she had liked him more and more; he was so giving, and uncomplaining, and natural, neither taking advantage of nor being overwhelmed by his introduction into the Vicarage in a way that experience had taught her was rare, and she had hoped that in time she might be able to help him in more ways than just his drawing; she recognized that in her lonely life she had come to get fond of him in a way that was rather more than a teacher's affection for a good pupil. Now she had hurt him in a way he had done nothing to deserve, because of her own unhappy feelings. And while she recognized all this, at the same time she knew that she was being ridiculous, bothering about hurting a farm urchin's feelings. Her own father would have clouted him in the same circumstances and considered he had got off lightly. By the time she had straightened out her own dreadfully muddled emotions, and found herself calm enough to proceed, Tom was drawing the fern again, and Netty was back at her scales. May felt exhausted.

'Really, I do expect you to work when I'm out of the room, I can't be watching you all the time.' Her voice was merely grieved. She did not know it, but this hurt Tom more than her anger, which he knew he had done nothing to deserve. He did not look up, his eyes fixed on the fern.

'And you, Netty, its wrong of you to waste Tom's time. I've no doubt you were to blame. He spends so little time at his drawing. There, Tom, you've scarcely started.'

'He's done a lovely drawing of Ferdy,' Netty said boldly, not caring. Genuine female behaviour, Tom was thinking acidly, tale-telling . . .

'Show me,' May said.

Tom handed her the drawing of the cat. May, frowning, took it, and her face softened immediately.

'Why, that's exactly Ferdy! You've caught his expression – and that's very difficult with an animal. That's very good, Tom! Of course, it's not what I told you to do, but . . . well, I shall keep this. Now get on with the fern.' Her voice could change in its uncertain way from soft to sharp like a musical instrument.

Tom was so tired that the fern seemed to him like a jungle plant growing larger and larger before his eyes.

'And you, Netty –'

'Can I have a dog?' Netty asked.

The inconsequence of the question caught May off guard.

'Why, really –'

'*Please*,' Netty said. 'You've got a cat, haven't you? You wouldn't be without him, would you?'

'But you'll only be here for two or three years,' May said. 'What will you do with it when you go back home?'

'Take him with me, of course.'

'Don't be pert,' May said. 'Get on with your scales. I don't think you've done any work at all, for all the time you've sat at that piano.'

Netty had the nerve to groan out loud. Tom was full of admiration. But of course she was part of the family; if he were to groan it would be like cheeking Mr. Pettigrew. He drew on valiantly and Netty went back to her scales. May took care that they never shared their lessons again.

6

'I've found her,' Rebecca said.

'Found who?'

'Netty Bellinger, of course.'

Tim, preoccupied with what he had been doing, came out of his trance with a jerk. He had just come into the Vicarage kitchen after a stint at drawing Tom Inskip's view of Curlews, and was frozen stiff. Rebecca, recognizing a cold mortal when she saw one, put some milk on for coffee.

'Cripes, you don't waste much time!' he said admiringly. 'You haven't *met* her? She –'

'No. Not yet. That's all yours. It's your ghost, after all. I've just found her address.'

'How?'

'It's on the electoral roll. Not complicated at all. Miss Annette Lilian Bellinger, 46 Copse Road, Meldon. I looked in the Post Office.'

'But that's terrific! I thought it would be hopeless. I thought – oh heavens, have we got to go and visit?' The idea appalled him, suddenly – the Netty of the drawing being real. He felt they had been playing with the story, in a way, the whole thing being so far distant, its ghostly elements entirely acceptable; he felt curiously close to the short passage of Tom Inskip through the world in a way that he recognized as unnatural; he could not explain it and did not particularly want to. But now, if they met Netty, explanations were bound to follow. His own

Tom Inskip might become distorted; the story in fact might be grim, was bound to be sad. He felt distinctly uneasy at the prospect.

'Yes, of course,' Rebecca said relentlessly. 'You want to know what it's all about, don't you? We can go to Meldon on Saturday. There's a bus at ten. She's not on the phone – I've looked in the book.'

She looked pleased with herself, as well she might. She was formidably efficient.

'Fantastic luck, really. One, that she isn't married, so the name's still the same, and, two, that she still lives around here. I thought I would trace her in the end, through records, but I thought it would probably take ages. What have you been doing? Show me.'

Tim fumbled out his work and laid it on the table. He was distracted now, by Rebecca's news. Before he had set out, he had been distracted by his mother's. In between, he had forgotten everything but his work, irritated that sheer cold had hampered him. It was good, what he had done, but only a sketch for something he could see as far more involved. The intricate tracery of dead bracken alone, through which the distant landscape was seen as if through a screen, could take mornings, quite easily.

'No spider,' said Rebecca.

For a moment Tim did not see what she meant. Then he smiled. 'Yes, I know it is Tom's drawing. It was deliberate, in a way.'

'Only you've been taught better than Tom. Or else you're better anyway. It's really good.'

From Rebecca this was high praise. She did not pay easy compliments.

'Tom was just working in a vacuum, I suppose. I doubt if he had ever seen any real painting. He was good, but he had nothing to help him, not at home, and not much with Miss May, I shouldn't think. And doing hard physical work all day –'

'Not a man of leisure, like you.'

Tim smiled.

'How about you? Why are you off today?'

'I was actually given the day off, if you want to know. I'm doing a project on pollution.'

'You're making coffee.'

'Well . . .' She gestured to the table, which was covered with magazines opened at photos of dead fish, oiled seabirds, and bedsteads in rivers. Tim grimaced.

'That reminds me – '

'What?'

'My mother wants to move back to London. She says she's going mad.'

'Well, that's quick. Didn't she realize?'

'No. She was so bound up in making a new home she didn't think about anything else. I don't want to go back.'

Rebecca looked at him doubtfully. 'You'll have to.'

'I didn't want to come. Now I don't want to go. I'm what you call a conservative character.'

'A drop-out,' Rebecca said, less kindly.

'Well . . .' Tim shrugged. He still wasn't sure, only that advertising was definitely out. His mother's saying the grave picture was a good cosmetic ad. had decided all that. It only remained to fight it out, a prospect he did not relish. As bad as meeting Netty.

He sat down at the table with a shiver. Rebecca poured out the coffee.

'She doesn't even want to wait until spring,' Tim said. 'She's gone looking for flats already.'

'What does your father say?'

'He doesn't care. He doesn't like the journey. He only moved because she was itchy-footed. Now he just says it will have proved a good investment. He'll make money on it, so he's happy.'

Rebecca's lip was curling in puritan fashion at these capitalistic revelations. 'They are *the end*, your parents.'

Tim grinned. She went on morosely:

'You aren't going to tamely pack up and follow them back to some plushy pad with gold bath-taps in South Ken? But I suppose you've no choice? Do you want to?'

'No.'

'Have you told them?'

'No.'

'You must,' Rebecca said with relish.

'I told my mother I didn't want to go into advertising –'

'Oh, don't you?' Tim had forgotten that Rebecca didn't know this. 'Splendid!' For a moment, she looked like her mother. Tim, noticing, thought suddenly that she was after all in her family mould. Was he, too, for all his dreaming? He hadn't the excuse of being ill any more, for harbouring these unacceptable ambitions – or non-ambitions, to describe his state of mind more accurately.

'What did they say?'

'She wouldn't really listen. She wouldn't believe me.'

'You're too *tame*!' Rebecca said acidly.

Tim gave her a furious glance, the more furious because her jibe was true. 'Oh, cripes!' he said. He stood up, and started gathering up his work. 'You're quite right. I must get everything sorted out.'

'Now?' Rebecca said encouragingly.

'Yes.' He grinned. 'Just time for a quick cup of coffee.'

Rebecca's eyes were shining. She went to a cupboard and brought out a bottle of brandy, pouring a generous dollop into Tim's coffee.

'Medicinal,' she said. 'For courage.'

His mother was painting her finger-nails. Tim dropped his work on the kitchen table and said, 'Look, I've been thinking about this for a long time – I don't want to go into Dad's firm. I'd be useless doing that sort of thing. I haven't got his kind of brain. I want to do art.'

'Do art by all means,' his mother said coolly. 'It will be a fine training for your father's firm.'

'No. Not for his firm. Not advertising art. Proper art.'

'Art for art's sake.' His mother smiled. 'You are ridiculous, Tim! Do art by all means, but your A-levels are all decided. We had a discussion, if you remember –'

'*You* had a discussion. You and the Head. No one's ever asked me.'

'You've got a tongue, haven't you? You sat there like a moron the whole morning and never said a thing. You were thoroughly rude, and I felt very embarrassed. I put it down to your illness. If you didn't like what we mapped out for you, surely that was the moment to mention it?'

'Yes, it was, I suppose. I didn't really know what I wanted until quite recently, and now I'm still not sure – only that I won't set foot in Ingram's in any capacity whatever. It's not my thing. It's not that I'm ungrateful –'

'No?' His mother's voice was ominous. She got up from the table, holding her fingers out carefully. 'We'll talk about it tonight with your father. I've got an appointment in Meldon. I'm late already.'

Rebecca's brandy did not hold out until Mr Ingram got back from London. Tim, having had the whole afternoon in which to marshall his arguments, had none when the moment came. It was just back to the wall, stubborn, not losing his temper. He had not realized what it meant to his parents, his taking on the highly successful business that his father had built up from nothing. They used arguments that meant nothing to him, describing how poor they had been, how his father had slaved, how they had deprived themselves of everything in order that the business should thrive; how hard it was after the war, when everyone was after jobs, how competitive, how they lived in two rooms, 'and there was still rationing – one egg a week,' his mother said. Completely irrelevant, Tim thought.

94

'You've had everything on a plate, never wanted for the slightest little thing. You have *no idea* of the opportunity you want to turn down!'

'The best education that money could buy – with one purpose in mind, that you could carry on where your father leaves off . . .'

'I never *asked* for it!' Tim said. 'I can't feel grateful for having something I never wanted – '

He felt sorry for his father, in a way, sitting there with his cigar and coffee, and his face crumpled up into several chins and pouches and grooves, showing now all the evidences of the hard work he had put in, that he was so proud of. But his father had done what *he* wanted, after all . . . making the business work had been his own act of creation, far more dear to him, Tim thought privately, than his share in the creation of his own son.

'What is there for me, just to jog along running everything you've made, when I don't even think that way? I'd be useless, because it doesn't interest me.'

But not to be interested in the firm of Ingram's was beyond comprehension to his father.

'It's only yourself you're interested in,' his father growled. 'You've been spoilt, never having to want – you young people are all the same today. I've seen some, believe me.'

Who else had his father been interested in all his life, save himself? Tim wondered. His mother certainly took second place to the business, and was now going round the bend with boredom and what she called her nerves. Tim felt bad about upsetting them, but only in a strange, impersonal way. This slightly worried him too. Surely it wasn't fantastically selfish to want to decide for himself what he was doomed to spend his whole life doing? Not to have it decided for him against his will. 'When we go back to London,' his mother said suddenly, 'you will see things differently. This country business was a great mistake. There's no stimulus, no

95

entertainment, no competition. That and your illness – '

'I don't want to go back. I'd rather stay.'

'If you're not prepared to think again about all you've said tonight,' his father said, 'you might just as well get yourself a job. A few months of fending for yourself might make you see things in their proper perspective. Try farming. That's all there is down here. See how you like it, day after day, one heavy, boring job after another, year in, year out, no prospects of bettering yourself.' His father drew heavily on his cigar. 'Get out,' he said. 'The sight of you makes me sick.'

Tim thought he looked like someone imitating Winston Churchill. He went up to bed, and lay staring into the pitch-dark, listening to the wind in the elms. Had his father meant the last bit, about getting a job? It was hard to tell, in so charged an atmosphere. He felt miserable, and very alone. Friends at school had all this sort of thing with their parents – he had heard similar scenes described with enormous gusto and derision, and wished some of the same friends were a bit nearer, to laugh and clout him and fall about at the thought of him in the executive chair smoking cigars. Strangely, he hadn't missed his friends before. Rebecca, he realized, had become important to him, not as a girl, but as someone around who was on the same wave-length, no more. He could have done with her to talk to just then. She was so scathingly sensible and yet there was a peculiar brand of sympathy that emanated from her, as if she knew very well what it was all about. She was withdrawn and cold, and yet he felt that underneath her scorn and her reserve, there was, if not a heart of gold – no, Rebecca certainly hadn't got that – at least a fire of a kind, a fire tightly guarded, because her family was all sanity and reason and calm and turn-the-other cheek. He thought that she had screamed and had tantrums when she was little and her parents had been gentle, giving her nothing to bite on, soured her with reason.

He could not sleep. In the darkness, Tom's pictures, which he had pinned on his wall, gleamed familiarly. Tom knew all about farming for a living – is that what he had meant that day when the builder was there, standing by the fire-place saying, 'Mind it doesn't happen to you?' No. Tim remembered that that was his death, the ultimate story that on Saturday they might uncover.

Tim, in his great uncertainty, felt that through coming to Inskips, and particularly through Tom, he had formed this antipathy towards the life his parents had mapped out for him. He had no idea how much Tom's drawing meant to Tom, but he knew now that his own painting meant a great deal to him. He had drawn on Tom's vision for the things he had been attempting, and in these last few weeks of unaccustomed freedom he had discovered an excitement and a purpose in his painting which he had never felt before. It really was what he wanted to do, unbound by any commercial applications. And if that was impractical, as far as earning a living was concerned, he would rather do some potty undemanding job just for bread, and go on with the painting whenever he could. Of course, if his parents would forget their ambitions for him and let him go to art school . . . but that, at the moment, was not very likely. Whatever happened he was determined not to go to University. He knew he wasn't exceptionally clever – his good results were only the result of cramming and the very privileged educational processing mill that had put him through its machine. 'Brainwashing,' he thought. 'It's only doing to people what my father's firm does to goods – grooming them and making them saleable.' But it was so hard to *know* if one wasn't being a bit of a fool, rejecting it, when to Tom Inskip's generation it must have been a star beyond the wildest reach, to get a good education. Had Tom, who had proved he had more in him than just farming, ever wanted desperately to do something more demanding? Tim yawned, drained by his brain turmoil, and wondered whether a farm labourer's job would be bearable. His father was right when he said there wasn't much else.

The clouds had cleared and through the window a few stars were showing, hung up in the elm branches like Christmas lights. Christmas was very close – two weeks. It all had to be decided by the beginning of next term. The branches were creaking in the wind – nothing different there, from Tom's day. Tim shut his eyes, and saw the stars again, but paler now, the stars of a winter's dusk, shining while the sunset was still in the sky. There was a deeply rutted path going down to the farm, and thick bare hedges on either side. Bright lines of water gleamed in the ruts; a few crows wheeled raggedly across the horizon where the last light was hard and greenish-yellow with wind and winter and promised rain, and a solitary lamp gleamed in the kitchen window of the farm-house. In Tim's vision it was starkly beautiful and uncompromising, a night of hurry-for-home and fur-lined anoraks, a landscape in the Victorian style, like a long-forgotten Christmas card, an old painting in the Royal Academy, gathering dust. An empty cart was going down the lane heading for home, and a laden cart was coming up, the horse head-down, floundering and straining through the mud. Tom was at its head, shouting encouragement at intervals, floundering himself and catching on to the shaft to steady himself, mud up to the knees. He wore a cap and a flannel shirt with braces and a cotton scarf round his neck, a tattered jacket, and cord trousers tied with string round the knees. He looked tired but shouted to the other carter cheerfully enough: 'Last one!' The wind drove at him, spilling his words away; the other carter, perched high and swaying to the lurching progress, laughed and made some jibe. Out on the pasture the muck-heaps patterned the field, geometrically precise and tidy, and out on the still bare corner Tom delivered the last of his day's work, swearing every now and then when the horse, eager to be home, moved off too soon. Seven yards one way and nine yards the other, seven heaps to a load and ten loads to an acre . . . The Pettigrew farm was exactly worked, the men driven as hard as the horses, their needs cared for as long as they were in health, their rewards a bonus at Christmas and a harvest supper. A boy of fourteen was allowed two loads less than a man. Tom's stint was finished, and he drove back down the lane, sitting on the front shaft, warmed by the horse's steam and the clatter of his pitchfork in the empty cart. The smell of dung, rich and black as pudding, clung about his nostrils, the smell of good husbandry. And Tim, watching, was acutely envious of Tom's physical state, the untroubled mind, the bodily fatigue. It was simplicity itself. It was something he knew nothing of. Did he want it?

Tom was smiling, very close, very tired.

'Were you happy? Were you satisfied?' Tim wanted to know.

Tom just smiled.

He never had time to wonder, Tim remembered. It was over too soon.

Miss Netty Bellinger's house looked empty, even from the road. It had dirty net curtains at the windows, a garden run to riot, and bird-droppings all over the doorstep from a nest in the porch. When Rebecca rang the bell, it made a cracked forlorn noise inside, and nothing moved.

Tim was almost relieved. Rebecca was bitterly dis-appointed. She rang three times, and stamped round the back, but there was no sign of life anywhere.

'There's still furniture and stuff in it, though. It must still be hers. Let's ask next door.'

'She's gone away, love,' said the woman next door. 'They took her away, in fact. Poor old soul, she had a fall, bit of a black-out, a few months ago.'

'Where is she?'

'I couldn't tell you, I'm afraid. They took her to Oldbarn hospital, but later they moved her, so I heard. But I couldn't tell you where to.'

Oldbarn hospital was ten miles farther on, and Rebecca had to buy a hundred balloons, two hundred paper cake-cases, six biros and four electric light-bulbs for the Christmas disco at the Vicarage. They walked on up to the shops, the afternoon having suddenly taken on a very tame aspect. Tim realized now how very much he *did* want to know. The feeling of relief at the house being empty had just been a kind of funk, because for some stupid reason it mattered now so much.

'It's only curiosity,' he said.

'No,' Rebecca said, in her abrupt way. 'There's more to it than that.'

Tom didn't ask her what she meant. He thought she was right, but it was something he would not discuss.

'We'll do the shopping, go home, and ring up Oldbarn. They can't have lost her. We'll never get to see her before Christmas though – by the look of it. This ghastly party . . .' Rebecca scowled.

'I thought the party was a *fun* thing,' Tim said, amused.

'Not for me,' Rebecca said firmly.

Tim had promised to help Joe Morgan install the disco apparatus, and generally make himself useful; even his mother had agreed to go and fetch a batch of hot sausage-rolls from some willing but transportless cook out in the nether regions. ('After all she does nothing useful all day long,' Rebecca's mother had remarked to her husband. 'I'm sure it wouldn't strain her.') Rebecca refused to consider the evening as anything but a frightful bore. Tim, who enjoyed parties and dancing, decided he had never met a girl quite like her. At times the hedgehog prickles became positively porcupine.

As if to demonstrate this last fact, she now said acidly, 'We want to get it solved before you go back to school, else we shall never know. If your parents are going to move, I don't suppose you'll be back here again.' She didn't sound particularly sorry, only annoyed to be thwarted in her detective role.

'Who said I'm going back to school?' Tim said.

'Oh, you're bound to conform in the end,' she said scathingly.

Tim was silent. Time was running out; school started on the tenth of January and if he agreed to go back, he knew he would agree to everything else thereafter. Once back in the machine, on the University conveyor belt, he would never find the courage again to step off. Rebecca was not endearing, with her blunt scorn. She had brought him down to her level of depression, which was probably what she had intended to do. They did the shopping in silence and went back to the Vicarage to telephone Old-barn. Tim knew that he was pretty dull in the guts, and resented Rebecca's reminding him. While she telephoned, he sat on the stairs, staring morosely at her frizzy hair and shapeless jersey figure, pleased by her ugliness and her undesirability.

'She's still there. We can go and see her,' she said, putting the receiver down. 'Three to four any afternoon.'

Tim didn't say anything.

'After the party,' Rebecca said grimly. 'We'll go the day after. On Thursday.'

Tim liked parties. He wasn't particularly shy and he had already found out that girls found him perfectly acceptable, and that he could generally get involved with anyone he really wanted to, and he could dance quite well, and he liked drinking enough, so that everything became carefree and rather ridiculous and funny. He agreed that if one had the good fortune to have this particular mixture of talents, parties were bound to be good fun, but if you didn't – if you were shy, or couldn't dance, and drinking merely made you feel miserable instead of merry – they were more likely to be an ordeal. He could see straight away, on the night of the Vicarage disco, that Rebecca came into the last category.

'The trouble is I can't not go,' she said, 'because it's here. Normally I avoid them like the plague.'

'Why?'

She didn't answer. She wouldn't even wear a dress (and it occurred to Tim that he had never seen her in a skirt, except on her way back from school), only a pair of plum-coloured Levis and a skinny matching sweater. She put eye-shadow and mascara on – 'So that however miserable I am I know I can't cry,' she said. She smiled when she said it, but Tim guessed that she meant it.

'Cripes,' he said, 'talk about the life and soul! Does it always take you like this?'

'Yes,' she said.

'She'll grow out of it,' her mother said briskly, stating the great parent panacea for all ills, which Tim was familiar with himself. Rebecca's mother, dressed for a party in her own completely individual fashion – voluminous dark green velvet with gold chains and a hair-ribbon to match, like a nineteen-thirties literary critic – was counting the beer-bottles in the kitchen.

'Do let me know if you see anyone beginning to have too much,' she said to them both. 'So much better to find out beforehand, than when it's too late.'

How capable she was, and uncensorious, Tim thought, for a vicar's wife. Already the music, which most parents found unacceptable for a start, was blasting through the house at the required number of decibels, so that speaking in the hall and the lounge was impossible and even in the kitchen difficult. The Vicar was perfecting the lighting system, which was proving somewhat temperamental – although he insisted on calling it the 'darking system' instead of the lighting system. He could be seen in the hall, intermittently bright violet, a screwdriver in his hand. The lounge, warm for once with an enormous fire in the hearth, was satisfactorily dim and smoochy-looking, with several early enthusiasts making the most of the space to start their gyrations before the competition got too fierce. Loud motor-bike noises from outside punctuated any slight lull in the noise inside, and the party was obviously going to be very well attended. In fact, Tim thought happily, it looked like being a very good evening.

His own mother, arriving with her sausage-rolls, was given the job of getting about a hundredweight of potatoes into the oven to bake in their jackets. Tim was amused, noticing how competently Rebecca's mother got things done; he realized that she was as deep and as wise as his own mother was neurotic, and anything that Rebecca suffered from such a mentor was by default rather than misunderstanding. Rebecca was very far apart from her mother because they met so rarely. Her mother was so busy – and no doubt competent at – straightening out other people, that she perhaps didn't notice how badly her own daughter needed a little mothering. 'A secure home is everything. Rebecca is very lucky,' Tim could imagine her saying in her deep, well-educated voice, and not ever noticing, for all her profound intellect, her own daughter's blocks to happiness.

As Rebecca seemed determined to stay in the kitchen, Tim helped himself to a pint of beer and went out and found himself a cheeky little blonde to dance with and passed the next two hours in a most satisfactory manner. The place became very crowded. Nancy, the blonde, told him who everyone was, including the names of 'all the gang from school' (Rebecca's school, presumably) and ending with 'that tall dark boy, Rod, is who Rebecca is sweet on.'

'Never!' said Tim.

'Yes, really. We're all mad about him.'

Tim studied Rod, and recognized a lady-killer in bud, devastatingly gifted with looks and physique, and – to judge by the ease with which he found an audience – with charm, personality, and humour to boot. The girls were bound to fall for him, he realized, but Rebecca! For some reason he jibbed at Nancy's revelation.

'Not Rebecca –'

'She yours then?'

'No, but I didn't think she was interested –'

'Oh, grow up!' Nancy said scathingly. 'She breathes, doesn't she?'

All breathing girls apparently had to love Rod. Tim grew cool towards Nancy.

'Rebecca may be weird on top, but she's quite normal where it matters. She adores Rod. You ask her.'

Tim had some more beer, considered Nancy's proposition, and rejected it. He couldn't see Rebecca anywhere and danced with several more of Rod's cast-offs, and had some beer. Some time after midnight, coming back from the loo, he met Rebecca in the hall.

'Do have one of your mother's baked potatoes,' she said, frigidly polite. 'You've had too much beer.'

'So have you.'

'Yes. It's bearable then.'

She went back to the kitchen with him, where several people were milling round and the light had been put off, so that the fire glowed without competition, friendly and comfortable. Tim fetched some food on a plate and they sat down on the floor by the boiler, and Tim saw that Rebecca was crying.

'Your mascara,' he said. 'Bad for it.'

'Yes.'

'Never mind.' He thought of Rod, and the hopeless competition Rebecca knew she faced and offered her a baked potato, the only consolation to hand. 'Cripes' he thought, 'poor Rebecca!'

'Do you want to dance?'

She shook her head.

'What then? What to cheer you up?'

'It's impossible. I feel sick. I think I'd better – '

He went to the door with her and the night outside met them, incredibly fresh, a razzle-dazzle of stars and a moon swinging in the arms of the churchyard pines. Rebecca was discreetly sick in the shrubbery and came back shivering.

'I don't want to go back,' she said. 'Not in there. I wish I were dead.'

'Yes, but not constructive. What do you want? I'll stay with you. Don't cry. It doesn't matter.'

'It does matter. You wouldn't know.'

His mother's car was parked in the drive and he opened the door and said, 'Here, it's warmer.'

They both got in and shut the door.

'Let's go somewhere,' Rebecca said.

Tim hadn't intended this, but saw no reason why not, recognizing – even as he thought it – that the beer had got him. But no matter. Parties were for such liberating. Their elders and betters all did it, between lectures to their young not to. He started the car and they swung out of the drive.

'A nice fast road somewhere,' Rebecca said. 'Go out to the arterial.'

'This isn't anything to do with wanting to be dead? After all, I don't want to be.'

'No. I just want to see how fast it goes.'

Rod did it, he supposed. Magaziney Rod, with a fast sports car. Oh, well. After five miles he found the arterial, and put his foot down. This part was easy, easier than getting out from the post office between the letter-box and the pram. The beer made it seem easier still. The sober part of him was watching, but even that wasn't censorious, only very slightly worried in case . . . In case what? Just to cheer up Rebecca.

'Better?' he said.

They were doing seventy and she was watching the speedometer.

'No,' she said. 'It can't ever be better. Not when you're like me. Most of the time it doesn't matter, you can think about other things, but parties – that's what they're for – to get you all worked up and the inhibitions to go – dancing and all that – and drink – and saying things you wouldn't say in cold daylight. But when you're like me, it doesn't work. It's all no good, because of what I'm like – all these bloody freckles and hair like coconut-matting and saying all the wrong things . . . and freckles like saucers . . . The tears were pouring down her cheeks; Tim could see them shining in the oncoming headlights. He was watching the road, amazed, thinking, 'Cripes, she's drunk! She's crazy as a coot! What bloody freckles, for heaven's sake?' He had forgotten she had freckles. One just didn't notice things like that once they were familiar. She cared because she wasn't *pretty* – Rebecca of all people!

'Stop being so damned stupid,' he said. 'You –'

And then there was a wailing noise right behind and he saw the blue sign 'Police' through the rear mirror and looked at the speedometer. Eighty-five. Strange how you didn't notice in a good car. His father would be mad. Oh, cripes, and all because of Rebecca and her crazy freckles and that woodenhead Rod not loving her! He should have stuck to Nancy.

7

The day after, on the way to Oldbarn, their meeting was restrained and sore.

'What did your father say?' Rebecca asked.

Tim shrugged. 'Let's not talk about it. It didn't make things any better between us, put it that way.'

They sat in the bus most of the way in silence. It was crowded with Christmas-shopping women, and uncomfortable and cold after the magic ease of the Rover the night before. Tim was thinking, 'If I become an advertising hick I can ride in a Rover but if I become a painter it'll be buses.' He had been charged with driving on a provisional licence without a qualified person accompanying him and with speeding, and was lucky to have escaped drunken driving as well. Rebecca, after crying so bitterly before they had been stopped, merely laughed when the charges were listed, and had got a sharp dressing-down from a formidable policewoman. On the way home in the police car she had cried again, and got a lecture on the 'evils of the demon drink', but when they had arrived at the Vicarage – 'The *Vicarage*, did you say?' – she had laughed at the policewoman's obvious embarrassment at having to admonish a vicar. (Who had taken it very well, Tim thought – much better than his own father.) Altogether an up-and-down night, not very uplifting to consider in retrospect.

Rebecca was chastened and only said, when they were nearly at Oldbarn, 'I don't remember what I said last night in the car, only I know I was rambling on. What-ever it was, I didn't mean it.'

'You wished you were dead.'

'Oh, is that all?'

Tim remembered very well all the other things she had said but spared her the embarrassment of reminding her. She obviously had the gist of it still in her mind, for she said, 'Forget it anyway, whatever it was.'

Tim agreed to, although he knew he wouldn't. He felt much more sympathetic towards her, now she had revealed her frailty. Her flint armour would deceive him no longer. She was just as feeble underneath and rocked by circumstance as he was himself, possibly more so.

As the ten miles lurched past, he withdrew his thoughts from the disaster of the previous evening and diverted them to the prospect of Netty. This made him no happier at all.

'I don't particularly want to see her,' he said.

'You want to know, don't you?'

'Yes, but not to –' To what? He didn't want it shattered. He wanted it disclosed in the same way that it had been disclosed so far, by oblique twists and hints. Suppose Netty was ghastly? It mattered very much inside him; he felt that Tom's story was entirely to do with him. Not even Rebecca, for all her involvement. He did not want her ruthlessness to intrude here, among the ghosts. He thought Netty would be all right, but there was no guarantee. It wasn't *only* a story. There was more to it than that.

He could not answer Rebecca. He sat twisting the rolled-up drawing of Tom's grave in his hands. Rebecca had suggested they show it to Netty, in case her ancient memory needed jogging.

'She might be a bit gaga,' Rebecca had said.

'She won't be the only one then,' Tim had thought, acutely aware of his strange involvement with Tom.

'You don't believe in –' Rebecca hesitated – 'in – in rushing things, do you? Everything you do, you think about for ages first. You're so cautious.'

Tim agreed with the first statement, but not particularly with the second. If he were cautious, he would be an advertising man. Perhaps Rebecca had second thoughts, for she retracted.

'Well, not last night.' She smiled. 'That wasn't cautious.'

They got off the bus outside the hospital, and walked up the drive with all the other people carrying flowers and magazines and big hold-alls. Only two of this crowd headed for the Geriatric Ward, which was where they were to look for Netty Bellinger, and both of them were struck, quite suddenly, by what it meant to be old and not bothered with any more. It was very quiet in the corridor. They stood in silence, and Tim was filled with a suffocating panic at the thought of Netty Bellinger.

'Look,' he said, 'I don't want to see her. Not how she is now. You go and I'll wait for you.'

Rebecca looked at him in astonishment.

'Why ever –?'

'I just can't.'

Tim was so sure, that Rebecca recognized the fact and did not argue, merely shrugged and gave him one of her withering looks. Tim was quite surprised himself by the strength of his instinct, and sat down to wait on a bench against the wall. Rebecca took his drawing off him and disappeared. 'Now what?' he wondered. He was so curious about Netty and Tom, and all he had to do was follow Rebecca and find out, and he couldn't do it. He didn't know why. He had no constructive thoughts in his head, only an instinct not to probe. 'You are frightened,' he thought. Rebecca would find out and push it all at him and he would accept, then. It was the same as waiting for so long before deciding he wasn't going to follow his father. He was a friend of indecision, of not facing facts. Rebecca, sharp as a needle, would ferret and discover and file away in her rubber-stamp mind everything that crossed her path. She was going to be an oh-so-superb social worker, her casebooks full of facts and her trail littered with reeling, reorganized down-and-outs, stunned by her common sense. Tim stared at his feet. He really would have to decide something very soon. He felt inadequate and ashamed of his inadequacy, angry with himself and disturbed in his mind. Netty was too close. The whole thing was pushing at him.

When Rebecca came out she wore an expression of puzzled concentration. Tim did not say anything. She came up to him and said, 'It's no good. She's had a stroke and her mind is – it's gone away . . .' ('A hunting expression,' Tim thought, as she said. He saw the foxhound Mermaid, by Netty's side and the Netty of the drawing very real, very strong.) 'But she said' – Rebecca's expression was of deep concentration – 'I showed her your painting, and said it was Tom Inskip's grave, and she said, "Poor Tom. It was all my fault. Because of Mermaid." And then she wandered off and nothing else made any sense at all, except that she looked at the drawing later on and said, "The Queen of the Violets. May planted it, in the autumn." I asked her about May, but she just started talking about food and a whole lot of rubbish. It was useless.'

Tim was silent. It was enough. He hadn't wanted to know yet, and he didn't. He wanted Tom's presence to stay, as it did, in his other consciousness, to draw on, to use; he needed it, and when Tom's story was unfolded, which he knew it would be in its own time, he thought Tom would leave him. Tom, after all, was only a ghost, a figment of his imagination, little enough to want, little enough to draw inspiration from. Tim knew perfectly well that none of his feelings would stand up in the cold light of verbal examination; if anyone asked him how

110

Tom's ghost affected him, it would be impossible for him to say. It was a sense that haunted him rather than anything tangible, a sense of the irrevocability of what had gone before, of life proceeding generation by generation, the one before shaping the one after so that there was a responsibility to follow through one's own potential because it had been built up from all that had happened earlier. And in this argument, he felt he owed it more to Tom than to his father – Tom whose own potential had never stood a chance, its struggling chopped by some arbitrary fate that Netty now admitted was her fault. Tim was glad he had obeyed the instinct not to meet Netty.

'You can tell,' Rebecca said, subdued, 'that she has been rather spectacular in her time. For all her being potty now, you can feel that she has a very strong character. She has magnificent eyes – her face is all thin and fallen away and the eyes are dark blue and sharp – hawky, and the hair a great bush, snow–white . . .'

'I hate her,' said Tim, 'if it was all her fault.'

Eyes like wet violets, as it said about Molly, the musician's daughter, in *Household Words*. Again Tom was a bit dubious about the simile – *purple* eyes? – But could think of no better, staring at Netty while May listed her instructions for the night of the Christmas dinner.

'. . . help Matthews with the carriage horses, Tom – he's more gardener than groom and he's worried about it, although I can't think why. And then it will be your job to keep the fires going well – there will be fires in the dining-room, the drawing-room, the hall, the study, and the two main bedrooms, and if Mrs. Symes wants anything done she will ask you, so don't just disappear between whiles. Did Mr. Pettigrew give you permission to leave early? Then you can help Matthews with the lamps outside.'

'Mr. Angus said I could leave at three, miss.' Tom removed his eyes from Netty, who was copying some music into a manuscript book, and obediently fixed them on Miss May. The position of odd-job boy at the Vicarage for the night of the vicar's Christmas dinner (the bishop was invited) was supposed to be a privilege but, apart from the privilege of seeing Netty, which was rare these days, Tom could not see it. He had never shared his lessons with Netty since the night of the potted fern, and only glimpsed her in passing. His mother thought it a great honour for the family that one of their members should meet the bishop ('That old windbag,' said his father. 'Bad as Bellinger himself.') But Tom thought it more likely that he would meet the bishop's carriage horse than the bishop himself.

'They only want you because Bellinger's too mean to pay a man for the night,' his father said.

His mother said, 'Don't be unfair. Miss May has done a lot for him – he owes it to them, to help if they ask.'

'Meddling in lady's drawing is no help to Tom. Make a milksop of him.'

Tom had laughed at this, his line of thought being more after his father's than his mother's, and his father had grinned too, the two of them in league against women and their goings-on. Tom in fact did find pleasure in his drawing, now that he had Miss May's encouragement but, like his father, he thought it was a waste of time, and the fact that he derived this curious creative satisfaction – even excitement – from some of the results did not make him alter his opinion. His real work was on Pettigrew's land, doing what he was told and taking home his ten shillings, money which was badly needed. Tom was the only wage-earner besides his father and there were two baby sisters to feed, as well as a grandfather and an elderly spinster great-aunt to help out. Drawing was mere indulgence in their circumstances. Miss May could not see why he did not draw in his 'spare time', but Tom had never known 'spare time', as time at home was occupied almost entirely by such tasks as wood-chopping, weeding, fetching water, seeing to the pig – if not for his mother then for the old people. When everything was done he went to bed and even then it was hard enough to get up the next morning, to do everything all over again. Spare time was something he had never heard of. Miss May thought he was making excuses. Sometimes, when he arrived at the Vicarage for his lessons and saw the cook taking the remains of the supper out of the dining-room, back to the kitchen, he realized that Miss May very likely did not know what it meant to be hungry either, if that was what she sent back. He could hardly bear to look, his mouth watered so: pheasant, and treacle sponge, the syrup running into the sponge to turn it dark and moist, still steaming, and the custard almost untouched in a big silver bowl – once it had made tears come into his eyes, and he had had to go out and wait till the cook was finished and the velour cloth was back on the bare table. Potatoes and one square inch of bacon was all he had had for supper, and bread and lard out in the field at midday. The dark, treacly sponge haunted him all the evening and he could not draw.

'And make sure you're perfectly clean, especially your finger-nails.'

Tom blushed scarlet, because of Netty. Muck-spreading was over now and they were hedging. He was more likely to be decorated with thorn scars than to smell of dung, but he said nothing. Netty was smiling.

May, in one of her sharp moods, saw Netty's smile and said, 'And you practise your piece, Netty. Your uncle will ask you to play, you know, and the bishop is a fine pianist himself. You mustn't let us down.'

Netty made a face and Tom sympathized. At least he never had to draw in public. Miss May now separated them, Netty to the piano, and Tom to the study, where he drew for the rest of the evening to the strains of 'The Last Rose of Summer'. Outside it had started to snow, and when he went home he made the first footsteps down the lane, silently huddled against the soft wet flakes which were already drifting between the gaps in the elms. Pettigrew's bailiff, Mr. Angus, saw no reason why hedging should stop for a drop of snow. The grudging permission for an early departure on the day of the party, three days before Christmas, was granted, but when Tom left he wasn't, in fact, very keen to exchange his day's work for the womanish chores that awaited him at the Vicarage. There were worse jobs than hedging in the snow, dragging down the discarded wood to make great bonfires, and slipping gleaned potatoes into the embers to warm their stomachs with an hour later. It was already going dusk at three, and the bonfires were suitably festive against the iron-dark hedges, layered and trimmed and woven with meticulous workmanship to divide the acres. Tom was all woodsmoke and thorn tears. His mother went at him in the scullery with carbolic and brush: he shivered and squealed like a chased pig, regretting bitterly the shedding of his comfortable grime, but the brush attacked even his neck and the very corners of his ears and the roots of his hair – his scratches smarting abominably – and then a starched shirt, cold as a shroud, and a stiff Sunday collar . . . 'But I'm doing the horses! Not waiting on table!' . . . Thump, bang. 'Stand up straight! The *bishop* . . .' 'Blast the bishop,' thought Tom, mourning the hedging fire and the crumbly smoking insides of the burnt potatoes, even the billhook blisters scrubbed clean away. 'Be a credit to us.' Crash with the hairbrush on his scalp, a salty rag for his teeth, a clean handkerchief – 'Oh, Ma, leave me! I'll be late!' – and at last away down the lane, running while his mother was watching, and then slowing once the bend was past to a snail's pace, disgruntled and put out. It was snowing again softly, without wind, and the earth still and silent as if it had died, the bare trees stark, a robin dipping to him from frozen ivy in the hedge. Bishop's weather, he thought, austere and bitter, muffled in surplice white, ice patches glazed blue like church glass . . . The last of the hedging fire made a glow over the horizon like the sun going down, but there was no sun.

'Bother you, Miss May. I'd rather stay away.'

This, after a moment or two for composition, he said out loud, and his breath smoked around him. He heaved a great sigh at his plight, with splendid effect, and came to the Vicarage, glowing with lights through the trees, the great yews black underneath as a rook's wing but weighted with snow above so that they hung over the lane, brushing the railings. Tom sighed again, and went to report for duty.

So much for his best shirt . . . By the time he had got hay in from the barn for the visiting horses, bedded down six stalls and swept away the snow from the paths and the kitchen yard, fetched logs to fill all the scuttles, lighted twelve paraffin lamps, broken the ice on the trough, gone two errands for the cook, once to the village shop and once to borrow another saucepan from Miss Tweedie's next to the school, and cleaned the vicar's best shoes, he was no smarter than when he had come in from work. At seven o'clock the visitors started arriving and his work was outside – to light the gateway and direct the motley collection of vehicles to the yard, or help them to turn round if they were going home to call back later. He supposed one of them was the bishop, but could not tell in the confusion; the paraffin lamps showed him several bishop-like gentlemen all in black, helping their ladies out of their carriages, with much concern about hems getting wet in the snow; small avalanches kept descending from the laurels, so that Tom had to fetch an umbrella; then there were several horses to be seen to and the grooms to be shown to the tack-room where a fire had been lit and a cautious quantity of ale supplied. By the time Tom was free to go into the house, the dinner was well under way, as far as the dessert, he judged, by the jellies and caramel creams and fruit dishes going in on large silver trays under the cook's stern eye. The light and the warmth in the hall dazzled him. The two hired maids sharply chivvied him away, seeing him shedding snow on the doormat, and the cook, to get him out of the kitchen, told him to see to the fires.

'The dining-room one needs stirring up,' said one of the maids. 'What with all those bare bosoms – they'll be getting the goose-pimples!' They giggled together; the cook threatened to knock their heads together, and Tom was dispatched sharply to the dining-room. He went reluctantly, feeling a gawk in such company, but of course no one took any notice of him. They were all very talkative round the big table, lit by candles for the occasion, and heaped with dishes enough for Buckingham Palace (and plenty of port, Tom noticed); the ladies' dresses glowed with colour between the sombre blacks of their partners and, although they were mostly old and frumpish, Tom had only seen such glamour before in his mother's papers, such a sparkle of paste diamonds and tortoiseshell combs and long white gloves. He was impressed, almost excited by the picture, and stole furtive glances from his place at the hearth as he shoved more apple-logs into the fire. He pretended he wasn't looking for Netty, but he knew he was. She was sitting facing him, framed between the back of Mr. Pettigrew and the vicar of Meldon in such a way that she looked like a candlelit portrait, very serious and still among the chatter. For the first time Tom saw that she was no longer a little girl; she wore her imperious expression which, together with a low-cut dress of deep ruby velvet and the great red-gold halo of her magnificent hair, Tom found completely stunning. He stared, and she stared back at him, and he dropped the tongs in the hearth with a clatter, feeling as if the fire had come out of the grate and licked him. After that he dared not look again, but he sensed that she was still watching him, and the fire went with him all the way to the door as he made his retreat.

He did the rest of his chores in a dream. The cook gave him some leavings in the kitchen, and he helped himself to some dregs of port when she wasn't looking, and by the time 'The Last Rose of Summer' could be heard in its now fairly fluent version from the drawing-room, he was feeling quite pleased with his evening. He didn't think it compared very favourably with the Harvest Supper, which was a far less inhibited affair and his own particular standard of what a party should be, but he had no complaints about the food.

'And when you've quite finished,' the cook said sarcastically, sweeping a plate of trifle from under his hand, 'you can do the bedroom fires, for when the ladies fetch their cloaks, and then you'll be free to go back to the stables.'

Tom carted the logs upstairs and was on the landing, ready to come down, when the drawing-room door below opened, a great chattering and laughing billowing out with it, and Netty came out alone. She shut the door behind her and came across the hall to the foot of the stairs. She no longer looked imperious, but flushed and excited, her eyes shining, quite childlike again, in fact. She looked up at Tom, her face framed in the gold and crimson of her hair and dress in such a way that Tom was completely transfixed by her glory. In all his plain earthy life he had never seen a being to compare with Netty as she was at that moment (although, behind the port and the trifle and the firelight and the festive atmosphere, a little voice was saying somewhere: 'It's only Netty Bellinger. She's horrid underneath!') She stood, plainly waiting for him, and Tom felt himself going down the stairs, very slowly, dragging the empty log-basket behind him.

'Tom, what do you think? Something lovely has happened!'

She had a necklace of tiny seed pearls that sparkled in the lamplight, which Tom fixed his eyes on, feeling that her face was a fire that would burn him again.

Netty said, rather anxiously, 'Is something wrong?'

He shook his head, on a level with her now, which for some reason made everything a little more normal.

'Don't go away,' she said. 'I want to talk to you. It's such a bore being polite all the evening and minding one's manners so dreadfully, and that horrid piano-playing – ugh! But listen – here, sit here a minute, there's nothing to do any more, surely?' She had flounced herself down on the stairs, pulling her skirt close so that there was room for Tom to sit too. 'Sit down,' she commanded, so that Tom could do nothing but obey. 'Listen to my lovely news! Mr. Pettigrew is going to give me a hound to walk. You know what that means? – to look after until it's old enough to join the pack –'

Tom knew more about it than she did, but didn't interrupt.

'There's one called Mermaid that a farmer across at Robinson's is walking, and the farmer is sick or something and hasn't the time for it, so Mr. Pettigrew said would I like to have her until next autumn. May has agreed because it's not a permanent arrangement, and I can go and fetch her tomorrow. Isn't that lovely? I shall have a dog for my very own – until next winter, anyway, and even then I can go and see her. And I can go hunting and see my own hound working in the pack – isn't that a nice thought?'

'Yes,' said Tom. It sounded very inadequate, very quiet and hopeless. He cleared his throat. 'Very nice.'

She laughed. She had a great bellow of a laugh for a girl.

118

'So it was worth it – this boring old party. You can draw Mermaid for me, a portrait. Like you did of Ferdy. You're very good at animals.'

He could feel her gaze on him, candid and compelling. He lifted his eyes, and felt her interest and excitement shift from thoughts of Mermaid to himself, almost as if a beam of light had come to rest on him.

'We could have some splendid walks with a hound to take,' she said. 'Do you have to work all the time?'

'Of course I do.'

'It seems an awful bore. I'd rather do hound walking with you than with anyone else.'

Tom felt himself glow inside, as if the beam of light had gone right through him. He knew perfectly well that she had no other companions apart from Miss May, so that the comparison did not, seen coldly, carry much weight, but it was a lovely thought.

'There's only Sundays,' he suggested hopefully.

'Oh, Uncle Jim wouldn't let me enjoy myself on a Sunday,' she said. 'But there's hours in the week – after lessons, and spring coming, we could –'

What she thought they could do Tom never discovered for suddenly there was a large man in black breeches and stockings standing over them, looking like a crow, Tom thought. A cold breath of doom came with his shadow. Tom scrambled to his feet. With his log-basket and the smuts all over his hands he looked very much the servant, and – with one glance at the man's expression – felt it.

'Netty?'

In that one word Tom recognized surprise, distaste, and censure. Netty must have recognized it too, for her lovely glow was extinguished, a firefly pecked by the crow. Tom saw her shrink and flush up, just as he knew he was doing himself, and he thought how guilty they must look, as if they had been caught kissing, not just talking about dogs. It was because the bishop's one word accused them, its inflection suggesting something dirty.

Afterwards, when it was all in ruins, and he dismissed to his proper place (the stables) with words that were more painful than blows, he began to think that Netty wasn't lucky for him. It had been Miss May before, creating a situation where none was meant, now no less an eminence than his grace the bishop, with ungodly suspicions in his gaze. For the first time in his life, harnessing up horses in the cramped yard with the snow coldly pawing his face, icy fingers clumsy with the buckles, he felt a deep resentment against his lot. Not merely a crossness after being rated or banged about by his elders and betters, which was common enough, but a painful, deep anger. He was confused by it, and felt strangely bitter, almost sick. He knew he was 'gone' on Netty, but he could accept that without rancour, even knowing it could bring nothing but disappointment, but for the very first time he was angry with his inferior lot, pointed by the bishop's displeasure. If he had been that milksop, the son of the vicar of Meldon, the bishop would have smiled at his conversation with Netty, and wished them good night kindly. But he, with his potato hands and muck-rake blisters, his smuts and log-basket, must keep in his furrow, and touch his forelock, and know his place. Tom hit the bishop's horse across the nose for its fidgeting and then, remorseful, let its bearing-rein down by several holes to ease its lot. 'You poor old nag!' The horse was himself, in harness, working for its masters. So much for his 'education' at the Vicarage, and his useless drawing.

When all the horses were gone and the yard swept up and the lights extinguished down the drive, he went out under the snow-heavy yews and made for home. The last light went out in the Vicarage as he went through the gate, and the deep snow met him, thick and silent as death. The cottage was cold, his parents long in bed and the fire fallen to ash, hastened as usual by his father's good night douse of cold water. Tom crept upstairs and shivered into bed, his spirits in ashes too.

In the morning his mother asked him if he saw the bishop.

'Yes, he spoke to me.'

His mother's face beamed with satisfaction. 'There, now! That's what good connections do for you! Isn't that what I said? Isn't that what I told your father?'

Tom smiled, but did not say any more.

Mermaid came to live at the Vicarage. Tom saw her more often than he saw Netty. Once Miss May made him draw her for his lesson, but she was such a wriggling, bouncing, boisterous creature he could make nothing of her portrait. She lived in the stables, but Netty took her for long walks and very occasionally Tom saw them, a whisk of eager white and tan through the hedges and the gay orange-brown of Netty's everyday coat leaping behind. (Netty was a very unladylike girl, with none of Miss May's proprieties to bind her behaviour, Tom noticed. He had heard a few of the village women remark upon this with disfavour.) Otherwise he saw Netty in church on a Sunday, not very well for she was always in the front pew with Miss May while he, from habit, was well at the back, and always first out. It was no good waiting about, for he dared not speak to her in public, although she was game enough to wave at him without embarrassment if she saw him. Tom loved her distantly, cheerfully, and was not disturbed. The bishop he despised, and when he remembered the night of the Christmas party it was with sheer bliss at the recollection of Netty's closeness on the stairs, and the way she had looked at him. He forgot the bishop, his nature being one of pure optimism.

He continued attending Miss May's lessons, always

hopeful for a glimpse of Netty. As the evenings drew out, he was sometimes able to arrive at the Vicarage before dusk and one evening, as he came through the shrubbery, he saw Miss May coming across the lawn in front of the study windows, carrying a spade. The spade was rather unexpected, for Martin did all the gardening, but it was the expression on her face that made Tom hesitate – in fact retreat, taking a pace backwards into the cavern of the yew branches. He knew his limitations, and felt at a complete loss to approach such grief. The light was on in the study and the curtains undrawn, and for a moment May's face was illuminated, else he might have thought he was imagining it. She never looked exactly happy, but now she looked utterly bereft, torn with sadness. Tom was astonished by it, feeling that it must mean a death at least, and wondering whose death in her circumscribed life could mean so much to her, discounting her father, whom Tom did not think even his own daughter loved, and Netty, whom he could under no circumstances at all envisage dead. There wasn't any-body else. He waited until she had gone in, and followed nervously. For once Netty was there, in the kitchen. Tom looked at her anxiously.

'What's wrong with Miss May?' he whispered.

'It's Ferdy,' Netty said.

For a moment Tom could not even think who Ferdy was. Then – 'Her cat. Mermaid has killed it.'

Her cat! Tom gasped. 'The *cat*!' Grief as he had witnessed it was not for animals, not by Tom's reckoning. It was for – Tom's mind groped. Had he imagined it? It was how he would feel for Netty. He looked at Netty starkly. No, he had not imagined it. He felt very sober, his pity for May sharp enough to hurt.

Netty's face was both awed and excited by the incident. She had shed no tears, Tom could see by her face, and she was kneeling in front of the fire, holding an unrepentant Mermaid round the neck.

'Just one bite,' she said quickly. 'I couldn't do anything. Snap, like a crocodile. I – I couldn't –' She scrambled up, confused. Tom could see, with her using the word crocodile, that she was very close to being amused, proud of Mermaid for being so final. As if she sensed that she had given herself away, she hurried on, 'I know it's all wrong for hounds to go for cats – I couldn't help it. I beat her. Really hard, not just a slap. It's part of her training, you see.' Her eyes were sharp on Tom, and glinting. Tom knew that if he had sympathized, even smiled, she would have laughed. Had she seen May's face? The little drama had strung her up; she had no thought for May. Tom was still appalled by the starkness of May's face, and hated Netty's heartlessness.

'I was right to beat her, wasn't I? It was awful having to beat her.'

But Tom could not side with Netty. He did not even want to speak to her. He went on, without saying anything, down the passage and into the study where May was putting out his drawing things. He did not know what to say. May looked quite ordinary now, almost bright. But Tom could not forget what he had seen. He felt deeply drawn to poor May and did his best to please her but he could not get out of his mind the brief vision of her face on the lawn, like stone.

Some jobs were more wearisome than others, and the one Tom hated the most came with the spring – chopping out the ten-acre field of sugar-beet. The field was long and narrow, one boundary formed by a stream and a bank of willows. Tom was working on the stream side, and Arnold and two other boys were working at the far ends, too far away for talking to, so that the dreary job was even more dreary than it might have been, jabbing out the surplus plants to leave one tuft of bright leaves every eighteen inches – no more, no less, like the dung-heaps, for Mr. Angus was a mathematician when it came to the patterns of his crops. Tom felt the day stretching ahead, as uneventful as a cloudless sky, movement minimal, excitement nil, monotony every slow yard of the way until knocking-off time. This feeling was not at all uncommon to Tom. He accepted it philosophically, but it did not stop the pangs of regret leaping at intervals in his bloodstream. He was only fifteen and had another fifty years of hoeing sugar-beet every spring: one required a philosophy, unless one was dull enough to be satisfied. Arnold was talking of joining the Army. Tom didn't fancy the Army. He didn't know what he wanted half the time, and knew that he had no choice besides. Only – jab, twist, jab, jab, sniff, spit, jab – he hated ten-acre fields of sugar-beet.

The stream was cheerful with spring rain and the big blue willows rustled softly, their shadows skating and flickering across the bare earth. The air was warm, shivering with lark song. Tom, jab-jabbing, saw a water-rat in the reeds and a pair of moorhens making a nest, and the silver flash of a trout's belly. He had to look at the sugar-beet and not think, three hours gone and another seven to go.

The moorhens took off suddenly, in their clumsy half-run, half-fly, beating the surface of the water. The rat was gone, and the trout away with a quick flick of its tail. Tom saw the familiar pied, eager shape of the foxhound Mermaid rooting down the bank, the cause of the quick evacuation. He stopped in his hoeing, catching his breath for a moment, conscious of the blood running faster. He watched her, not wanting to turn round. Was she on her own? Sometimes she got out and hunted all on her own, chasing anything that ran. He cut out three more plants, trying to calm himself, and turned round.

Netty was on the other side of the stream, watching him. She was walking slowly, trailing a long willow stick behind her, her boots and the hem of her dress all muddy. When he turned round she waved at him and hurried so that she came to the other side of the stream opposite where he was standing.

'Come for a walk with me!' she shouted. 'It's much too nice to work!'

'I can't.'

'Why not?' she shouted.

Tom paused. She was standing there grinning at him, daring him, her face bright with the wind.

'There's primroses in Hanging Wood. I'm going there to get some for May. Do come! No one will know – you can be back before they know! Oh, it's much too nice, Tom –'

She twirled round, her long hair flying out, letting go of her stick so that it came across the stream like a dart towards Tom. He knew he was lost, although he tried, spearing three more inoffensive beets so viciously that he made three big holes in the ground. Netty started to walk on, swinging her skirt on purpose, laughing back at him. He could see how she was taunting him quite plainly, and he could see himself, the potato-faced farm nincompoop at his lowly peasant's job, no mind of his own to do what he pleased. A kind girl would never have asked him, or even come by him, but he knew now that Netty wasn't kind. She was all sorts of other marvellous things, but she wasn't kind. The sun was suddenly very warm, and the larks kept going up from the ground as if they were too full of song to remain earth-bound, and Tom, in that moment, felt much the same, with Netty's looks goading him and Mermaid leaping on ahead across the field as if to show the way. He stuck his hoe in the ground and jumped across the stream, and heard Netty laugh. He ran, and Netty was running too, ducking under the trees, stumbling and letting out little shrieks. Tom went past her and down the trodden path through the beds of willow-herb, running now because he had to run – it was in all his being like the lark's song, kicking in his heels, down through the mud where the cows drank and up the other side through the nettles and the elder bushes and the thistles, all the stuff that he would later have to cut back and tidy, if he didn't get the sack first. Mermaid streaked ahead, faster than Tom, much faster than Netty.

He got to Hanging Wood ten minutes before Netty, and sat waiting on the stile. He felt careless and wonderful, as if Mr. Pettigrew had personally given him a day off. He felt positively grateful to Netty, and watched her coming across the field with a sense of wonder at this feeling of release. He no longer felt inferior, because he was as free as she was. He could wait for her quite happily, smiling, seeing her for the first time with perfect freedom.

They went through the wood, picking primroses when they came across them, but only because it was an excuse. Tom knew that Netty had no thought of taking them back for May. She strung them like daisies, and put a string round her own neck, then round Tom's. They talked about lessons, and Netty's parents in India, and Tom's drawing, and May. Netty was quiet, her voice soft, her eyes looking away; Tom was surprised, having expected her to be boisterous and mocking in her usual way; a slight anxiety touched him, but faded in the same instant. They walked round the edges of the wood and came out on the long ride that led back to the stile where Tom had waited.

Tom did not know what he had expected of the escapade: in his eagerness nothing, he supposed. The freedom was enough. But as they walked back, Netty put out her hand and touched his. His own hand shied away, frightened, but hers followed and took it very firmly and held it. She still walked along, not saying anything, with the primroses round her neck, and he walked beside her, very carefully, feeling that the day had

126

come to a standstill. Their feet made no sound. The trees were thinning and the sun came through in shafts and splashes, and Tom found himself thinking that he wanted to get to the stile and nothing else to happen, just as it was now, no more, no less, because it was a perfect communication. It was something quite magical which did not belong to his ordinary life at all, and he knew by instinct that the moment was as fragile as a winter leaf's skeleton. Netty was more likely to spoil it herself than anything else: Tom had no great confidence in her subtlety. But she walked on, smiling faintly, and he fell in step with her, not wanting to break anything.

It was broken, of course. Tom knew that life wasn't like that really, and was not surprised. But afterwards he knew that if he had been lucky, the let-down would have been less violent.

They were about fifty yards off the stile when they first heard the sound of hoofs. It was ahead of them and approaching, coming along the ride they had taken when they first went into the wood. Tom hoped for a moment that they would get to the stile before the horseman appeared, but they were in no such luck: the horse was coming at a canter. Tom knew that the land was private, belonging to Mr. Pettigrew, and guessed that the rider was more likely to be Pettigrew himself than anyone else. If there had been any cover he would have hidden and dragged Netty after him, but there was nothing here except some thin and useless hazel; the great oaks brooked no undergrowth. He cursed, and they loosed hands by mutual consent, but walked on boldly. There was nothing else to be done.

The horse came round the bend fast, and Tom recognized its rider immediately. The horse shied at the sight of them, which was not surprising, but Pettigrew spurred it back on to the path and rode towards them at a brisk trot. He appeared to be in a hurry and Tom thought for an optimistic moment that he was going to sweep past –

he did, in fact, with a quick touch of his hat to Netty, but after the horse had broken into a canter again Pettigrew had second thoughts, for he brought the horse up, and turned in his saddle.

'Hey, you!'

Tom did not stop to hear more. Netty might be out for a perfectly legitimate purpose, but he was supposed to be hoeing sugar-beet in the ten-acre field, and Pettigrew knew it. Tom vaulted the stile and ran, leaving Netty where she was to answer Pettigrew how she pleased. He ran back as fast as he had come in the first place, but with a different urgency this time. It burned in his feet, and he was frightened, seeing all the consequences of his delightful freedom with a clarity he never suspected his imagination could rise to. In his mind he was working out his chances. The horse was Araminta, a bold hunter, and he guessed she would clear the stile without much difficulty if asked. A glance behind showed that Pettigrew was still talking to Netty, but another glance a few moments later confirmed the worst. Araminta was over the stile and the thud of her hoofs was in the turf beneath him. Tom ran, sick with foreboding. This was his job going, and his father's wrath to break over his head, a beating, his mother's tears. The blessed imagination gave him more speed than he knew was in him.

But Araminta, a flighty, unreliable mare, saved Tom from immediate doom. A pheasant went up from under her feet and she made it an excuse to shy again, violently this time, jinking off in the direction of home, for which she had been making in the first place. Tom did not see Pettigrew fall, but he saw Araminta wheeling round, riderless, and making back at a flat gallop the way she had come. Pettigrew was on his feet in a moment, waving his arms about and shouting. But Tom, delivered, was in no mood to return for punishment. He ran on, straight and fast as a fox from covert, and by the

128

time Pettigrew had chased and caught Araminta again, Tom had hoed out two dozen more sugar-beet plants, and was working on down his row with incredible zeal.

He did not speak to Netty again until the day of his death.

8

'Very well. That's it then. I'll say good-bye and leave you
to it.'

Tim, very polite, picked up his mother's suitcase and
moved towards the front door. He felt numb now that
the moment had actually arrived, and nowhere near as
triumphant at getting his own way as he had imagined he
would be. In fact he felt ungrateful, as his father had
decreed he ought to do during the very first argument.
But he was terrified now of letting any feelings show.

'You'll ring and let us know how you're getting on?
Remember you can come up any week-end, or any time
at all if you change your mind.'

'Yes, I know. I probably will some time.'

'And don't hold out just because of pride, if you change
your mind. The longer you stay here, the more you're
losing, all the time.'

'Gaining,' Tim said.

The one word guaranteed that his mother would leave
now without any show of sentiment. Her eyes went
frosty. Tim felt like a louse, but better that than going all
weak-kneed at the last moment. He put his mother's
suitcase in the car and she got in and he shut the door after
her.

'Look after yourself. Don't catch cold. Don't do anything stupid.'

He smiled. For one desperate moment he saw his
mother's face falter, but she had the sense to start up with

a roar and leave in a great splatter of gravel before the situation had a chance to develop, and with a great sigh of relief Tim was free to retreat indoors.

If he had been really certain that he was doing the right thing he would have gone in dancing, but, having stuck out through a really bad fortnight of desperate argument, which had involved his headmaster, the Dark Horse, the doctor, and a psychiatrist as well as his parents, he now in the moment of victory could not help feeling doubtful. His father had decreed – with a stubbornness as adamant as Tim's own – that if Tim was not going to use his education for following him in the family firm, he wasn't going to have an education for anything else. The Headmaster and the doctor both disagreed with this line, and suggested Tim should go back to school and continue his education with no obligations as to its future use. Tim knew he would have fallen in with this, in his weak and undecided state, and so wasn't sorry to have his hand forced by his father's pigheadedness. His father said he could leave school and earn his own living until he came to his senses and Tim had welcomed the suggestion and gone out the same day and got himself a job with Rebecca's blacksmith.

'And see how long you stick at that!' his father had bellowed at him.

His mother had wept. 'Just a common labouring job! How could you, Tim? After all we've done!'

Tim, pleased with his release for the time being, was no more sure than his parents how the experiment would turn out in the long run, which was the reason for his doubt. But with his father taking a flat in London, and now his mother's departure to join him, he did feel that he stood a chance of finding out. To be on his own – apart from a moronic housekeeper who was to come up from the village every day to clean the house and make him an evening meal – gave him an extraordinary freedom for a start. Not that he wanted to do

131

anything different; it was just a freedom of the mind, away from his father's gobbling pressure. He had never realized, until his father had gone away, just what a powerful influence he had exercised, merely by being there. Tim had always recognized his father's driving energy, his domination both at work and at home which amounted at times to ruthlessness, but he hadn't appreciated the effect of it upon himself, until the presence was removed. The sense of liberation was enchanting. The house without his parents was suddenly at peace, and so was he. For how long? Not very long, he guessed. He knew his father thought he would pack in his job after a week or two and follow them up to London; he had overheard him say that to the doctor when the doctor had said the idea was unwise. Everyone thought the idea unwise, except his father. And himself.

'I like it,' Tim said out loud, and wandered into the kitchen to make a cup of coffee.

Tomorrow he started work. Four miles there on the bike, four miles back and five pounds a week. It hadn't exactly been a bonanza to boast about, but at least it was a job and the metal-working part of it appealed to Tim. He knew he could do that sort of thing well. He wasn't sure about the horse part, though. Rebecca's Fred had been docile enough – if they were all like that he would manage, but somehow he thought that probably they weren't. Meanwhile, he had the rest of the day in which to paint, and no one to make comments, as his mother always did, nobody to tell him to mind the carpet, and not to take a best teacup for linseed oil. He found he was smiling to himself like the Cheshire cat. The life might pall eventually, but the beginning of it was marvellous. He felt so free of cares and responsibilities now that the decision was made that he felt he might float right off the ground.

Rebecca came down at seven o'clock to see if it had really happened. She had rarely come to his house before, because she could not stand Mrs. Ingram.

'I can't stay,' she said. 'I've got a load of homework. I just wanted to make sure –' She hesitated and smiled.

Tim said, 'All right. I know your opinion of me. You thought at the last minute I would have changed my mind and gone with my mummy.'

'Yes.' Rebecca looked a little embarrassed. 'Yes, I did.'

'So?'

'Up with you. Bravo and all that.'

'Thank you very much.'

He made her a coffee for a change. She sat on the table among all the paint, watching him.

'I'm going to see Netty again. Do you want to come?'

'No, I don't. Why, anyway? I thought she just rambled. What do you think you'll find out?'

'She might say something . . . last time she said it was her fault, and the Queen of the Violets.'

'What did that mean anyway, the Queen of the Violets?'

'The Queen of the Violets is the name of the rose on the grave. I asked Holy Moses, and I looked it up in a book on old roses in the library, and it was there, with a picture.'

'It must have been well looked after, if it was the one May planted.'

'Tom looked after it.' She did not smile. 'It's February the eighteenth in three weeks. I want to find out before then.'

'Your deadline?'

'Yes. Not for any particular reason. But it would be tidy.'

'Why should we find out? Does it matter?'

'Oh, yes.'

Tim did not pursue the theme, for it was the one with no answers that he had considered in the hospital. Rebecca was sitting on the table in a very drawable pose, he could not help noticing; he would make use of her, and change the subject at the same time.

Afterwards, when she had gone, and the drawing was

lying on the table, he thought it reminded him of something. He considered it, trying to think. It had come out quite well, and had a lively, surprised quality that made him feel the day had been well-spent. It reminded him of . . . the answer was there, but dodging him. He stared at it. Rebecca stared back. It was Netty, Tom's drawing of Netty –

'Oh, cripes!'

Tim felt as if someone had punched him. Tom haunted him more than he knew; the parallels had an inevitability about them that could be quite frightening if one let oneself . . . 'Oh, curse it!' He felt shaken. And more shaken by the extent to which he was disturbed. He was tempted to tear the drawing up, as if by that he could exorcise the influence. But Rebecca had not remarked upon any likeness – was it in his own mind? He had no idea. What did Tom have to do with him? If he let his imagination run riot, he would start getting worried about February the eighteenth. He glanced at the calendar. It was a Wednesday. Wednesday, a calm, characterless, mid-week, early-closing day. Perhaps he should stay in bed.

He started to put his things away, then remembered with a lovely jump of independence that there was no need to. He could leave them out and they could be all ready for the next time he wanted to paint. He washed his brushes and went into the sitting-room and turned on the television. He lay on the sofa with his legs up and thought, 'I can sleep here if I want to, without even undressing.' He didn't, but it was a nice thought.

Uncertain of how he was going to get on in his new job, the first days at it left Tim as uncertain as before he started. He could not say he liked it, any more he had liked lessons at school, but it left him each evening with a sense of satisfaction that was new to him, rather like doing a good drawing. He could not understand why, as during the first days he achieved nothing but a few stumbling successes in the removal of some loose shoes, a nodding, tactile acquaintance with some unfamiliar tools, the knack of lighting a cigarette from a hot horseshoe and the Christian names of a lot of men on tractors.

The forge was a large shed, open to a muddy yard and cold enough even when the fire was going hard. Tim quickly discarded his trendy gear in favour of some thick old wool and tweed, working-men's boots, a flat cap, and the embrace of the traditional smith's leather apron which came down nearly to his ankles. This, he soon found out when he started picking up horses' feet, was a purely practical garment.

'If you make 'em comfortable like, they won't jump around and then it's easier for you, that stands to sense,' George told him, as Tim gingerly experimented with a hairy, docile leg. At least he had quick, capable hands, and the mechanical jobs were easy enough. He made his first horseshoe on his third day at work and George was impressed by the result.

'I've had worse lads than you,' he commented, which Tim guessed was as far as he would ever venture by way of compliment. He was a man of few words, but quite amiable, and he passed on information with an instinct for what mattered and what didn't. If he saw that Tim was managing, he left him alone. Tim liked this. He had no complaints about the boss.

But the whole experience of his day now was something so strange to Tim that he wondered sometimes if it was really himself performing the round. The raw bicycle ride, a quick cup of tea, then the damp, hollow gloom of the old tin shed, the floor greasy with driven rain, spotted with fag-ends, the ashes of the fire spiralling up in the February draughts . . . if Tim, wondering, gave a momentary thought to the smug class-room of his public school or the streamlined offices at his father's place, it was as if his mind had moved to another planet. There was not any single facet of this new job that overlapped in any way at all with anything he had done before. He was conscious of this all the time, almost watching himself doing the new job, feeling his fingers on the sinews of the horse's leg, his cheek brushing the warmth of its flank, watching the fire with its new connotations – not as something to sit in front of, for comfort, but purely as a tool, its condition to be strictly controlled. He liked the practical challenge of working the iron; he preferred it to the actual shoeing, where the horse was merely an awkward, intractable but necessary reason for the work he enjoyed more.

Going home to his plushy, lonely 'spacious country residence of considerable charm' (it was now up for sale and so described in the local paper) he was acutely aware of the contrast between what he now did all day and everything else that had so far gone to make up his life. Going home, pushing the door open to meet the civilized, thermostatically-controlled airstream and the soft fitted carpets, the smell of his dinner in the oven, the gentle fluting chime of the ormolu clock in the hall recess, this contrast was so sharp that it gave him a sense of unreality, as if the whole thing were some joke escapade from which he would presently wake up. He realized that this was how his parents saw it. He realized too that he was, in a sense, cheating.

He tried to explain this to Rebecca. 'If I were a real blacksmith's apprentice, instead of just playing at it, I would be going home to some deadly box-room in a Meldon council-house and egg and chips every night. Five pounds a week wouldn't keep me in puncture outfits. I'm a subsidized labourer. I'm still depending on my parents.'

'It's a start,' Rebecca said sensibly. 'You can work up to a Meldon council-house, once you feel more sure of yourself.'

Tim was not so committed that he didn't think this remark very funny. Rebecca meant it in deadly earnest.

She really was all set to be a social worker, he thought sadly.

He yawned. He was too tired in the evenings now to worry very much about the whole thing. Perhaps that was why he had worried so much before – just having too much time on his hands. He would stick it out, he thought, even if it came to the council-house. Then, whatever he did, he was free from any sort of obligation. Rebecca, staunchly in favour of the straight and narrow as far as he was concerned, would strengthen him with her funny remarks.

'I went to see Netty yesterday,' she said. 'But she's ill, they told me. Failing. I couldn't speak to her.'

Tim did not reply.

'I'll try again on Tuesday. I've got three free afternoons next week – some old teachers' conference.'

'I've got Wednesday off. George is going to the races. He offered to take me but I thought a day off nags would do me good. If it keeps on freezing, I might try a bit of skating. Have you got Wednesday afternoon off?'

'Yes.'

'Fancy it?'

She looked doubtful. 'Skating? Where?'

'On the lake, I thought.'

'I haven't any skates. But I daresay I could borrow some. I might come.'

'The weather forecast says hard frost and no let-up for a week. They might be right for once. Skating on the lake would be marvellous, after Richmond.'

'It's very deep. No good unless it freezes really hard.'

'I'm not daft.'

'No?' She smiled. She was distant, almost preoccupied, and had a way of looking at him reflectively that he found slightly disturbing. He felt as if she had a casebook on him at home. He wasn't so hard up that it worried him, though. There was a bonus to the blacksmithery that he hadn't counted on: the girls that brought in the riding-school horses and the point-to-point horses. They were a tough, cheerful breed, who looked at males with the same quick eye that they used for a horse. Some were a bit too tough to his way of thinking, but the ones in his age range, the starters, provided several possibilities. They weren't shy, either. George had commented on this fact with his blunt tongue.

'You watch 'em, my lad. There'll be more lost shoes from that lot than pigeons in the corn if you give 'em any encouragement. Hard up for young men we are round here, that's the trouble.'

And yet Tim realized he would miss Rebecca if she wasn't around. Possibly she would miss him, although he doubted it.

By the Wednesday of the races he had had enough time for the job to lose its novelty and take on a more normal aspect; he could consider it more coldly, the pros and cons. He lay in bed most of the morning, considering, then went downstairs and tried to work out a design that he had been carrying round in his head, an almost abstract picture of the forge, based on the shapes and textures of the shed itself and the yard with its pattern of ruts and bright puddles. He had some sketches to work from, which he had done in his dinner-hours. This took him till two o'clock, when he fetched his skates from the garage and decided to walk out to the lake to see if the ice was good enough. He was pretty sure it would be, for it was still freezing hard. The races had been cancelled but George had decided to have the day off anyway. Tim wondered if Rebecca would come. It really didn't matter, either way.

He walked down the lane to the Vicarage, and cut through the churchyard. There wasn't a soul about. It was very still, not even a cobweb stirring, as if the frost had petrified the very air. Tim's breath hung in clouds and he could feel the drops of moisture on his eyelashes and dripping off his hair. If Rebecca didn't come, it wasn't waiting-about weather. He began to think, in fact, that it was more suited to staying at home painting.

He went down the churchyard to the wall, skirting Tom's grave with the same, odd feeling it gave him each time he set eyes on it, a sort of apology, a feeling of deep, personal regret. The old rose stood in a tangle of white hoar-frost, its trunk as thick as Tim's arm. The engraving on the stone stood out with a strange effect, because of the weather, and the date that Tim had had difficulty in deciphering in the first instance caught his eye now quite plainly, '18 February, 1910'. It then occurred to him, as if the message was there in the frost especially for him to see, that today was the Wednesday, the anniversary, the eighteenth of February.

The realization gave him a shock, a creepy feeling he could not deny, although his good sense at the same time told him there was no reason for it. This was the day he had thought he would stay in bed. But he was going skating. On a deep lake, his brain added. 'Mind it doesn't happen to you,' Tom had said. 'But I don't know what happened to Tom,' Tim thought. 'I don't know he got killed skating.' It was highly unlikely, in fact. Country boys knew all about when it was safe to skate and when it wasn't. Tim wished he had gone the road way, and not seen the date; it unnerved him in spite of all the good sensible reasons he could think of as to why it shouldn't.

'Tom, Tom,' he muttered. 'Don't haunt me.' But Tom was very close now, following him down through the dead bracken, grinning, swiping at the brittle white fronds with a stick. 'Imagination,' Tim thought. 'Blast Tom.' With a great mustering of British phlegm, he banished Tom out of his mind. He thought of strong, real things, like his father and Ingram's advertising, and the car he would like but now wouldn't be able to afford on a blacksmith's pay. The question kept going through his head: 'What am I going to do?' but somehow instead of being to do with his life it was to do with Tom. Tom,

139

following him, had put him off the idea of skating. But, because it was so stupid to be put off, he carried on down the long tumbled slope, the hoar-frost covering his jacket like snow, his boots crunching and snapping through the undergrowth.

The lake lay hard as stone, ringed by white trees and reeds like spears that cracked to a touch. There was no seeing under the glazed surface, no hint of the secrets and the life imprisoned far below. Tim doubted if it was solid, but pictured all the inmates of the lake getting pushed closer and closer to the bottom and to each other, the fish and the creeping things, the amoebae and the dead toads, the sodden leaves and decaying wood. He stood staring, as if hypnotized. Tom was very close, leaning against the tree, Tim thought, although he could not really see him, only feel his amusement. Tom had never been a miserable ghost, never even frightening: a purely amiable presence, unnerving now only because of the date and all the imaginings of Tim's own mind.

'You've come here to skate. What are you waiting about for?' Tim felt the question hanging in the air, but he could not tell if it was Tom asking it or himself.

'I'm going to in a minute.'

He dropped his skates down by Tom's feet and stood with his hands in his pockets, hunched against the cold, looking across the lake. A jay called from the trees up by the house, raw and screeching; otherwise the silence was intense. The ice, unflawed, took no sides for or against. It stretched across to the far slope, like polished iron under an iron-grey sky.

Tim had no excuse. He sat down on a mouldering log and slowly started to untie his bootlaces. He was wearing his working boots, heavy thick ones in case a horse trod on his toe again. It didn't look as if Rebecca was going to come now, and he would feel pretty stupid even to himself, let alone admitting it to Rebecca, that he had come down to the lake and not skated because the date unnerved him. In actual fact, he knew Rebecca would appreciate his feelings more than he appreciated them himself. He didn't want to be proved a coward quite so obviously, although he was quite happy to admit the fact in theory.

'No one need ever know,' he thought, pulling the skates towards him. 'It is terribly stupid to prove to yourself you're not a coward.' Or was it? Unresolvable. It wasn't fashionable to be heroic any more and to be a coward was perfectly acceptable socially. But one did have oneself to live with. Tim started looping up the long bootlaces of the skates. Strange how things changed in fashion, not just clothes but attitudes. Before he could swim very well he had been haunted by the hypothetical vision of himself standing on the edge of a deep pond (it could have been this lake) in which a child was drowning, and having to decide whether to try to help or just stand there sensibly not trying because he would only drown himself too. It was what had driven him to learn to swim and do life-saving, although he had no interest in either. But nothing had been proved either way, for the opportunity had never arisen.

He stood up and walked the few paces to the ice. He was a far better skater than swimmer and just looking at the ice for a moment with a purely professional eye it did strike him as very inviting. All other things apart. It was all very well becoming a blacksmith's lad, but he didn't have to take on the role of original village idiot as well . . . . After only another moment of hesitation he launched himself smoothly from the bank and the silence was broken by the hiss of the skates beneath him. He felt a surge of quite unreasonable excitement and started to skate with a glorious sense of ease and freedom, listening to the familiar, venomous passage of steel over ice with real pleasure. 'And nuts to you, Tom Inskip!' he said out loud, and the words made cold clouds against his cheeks.

If he had stayed longer on the bank, he would have

heard Rebecca coming far sooner. He heard her call, but thought it was the jay again – it was harsh enough, and broken with fear, but he did not recognize it. She was running down the slope from Pettigrew's, leaping and scrambling through the frozen undergrowth like a demented thing. Tim saw her before he heard her, and straightened up in surprise. He thought she had gone mad.

'Tim, stop! Don't!'

Exactly what he had thought a few moments earlier, but why Rebecca? She was in her school uniform, her long legs, all scratches, flying streamers of nylon. He skated towards where she was going to reach the bank, and was amazed by her appearance.

'Tim! Oh Tim!'

Whether she was sobbing from hysteria or merely for breath he never made out. He came to the bank and she flung herself on him, burying her face against his chest so that his face was blinded with frost-wet hair. He put his arms round her instinctively, to keep his balance, but then kept them there, amazed by her distress and genuinely concerned.

'What is it? What's the matter?'

'You – the date – oh, Tim, I thought – I thought –' She wept.

'Rebecca, stop it. It's all right, whatever it was. Nothing's happened.'

'It *was* the lake! I found out. I found out this afternoon – he was drowned in the lake, through the ice – and then I knew you –'

'Oh, Rebecca, don't!' She couldn't speak for tears, and he had to comfort her, holding her close. His instinct had been right then. Tom's ghost had known, of course it had known! 'Mind it doesn't happen to you' was almost the first thing it had told him.

'I got the bus – it was so slow! I was in agony! I got off at Pettigrew's – I thought it would be quicker. I ran all across their lawn, and I saw you – I saw you – I thought you would go through like Tom – I thought I was too late –'

She was shivering, cold as cobwebs in spite of her running. Tim said, 'But the ice is feet thick, Rebecca.' Even as he said it, he knew that nothing would get him back on the ice again, not all the common-sense in the world.

'But the date, Tim! Everything –'

'Yes, I know.' And Tom's presence, beating at the frozen bracken with a stick, following him down the slope. He would not tell Rebecca. It was all finished now, if she knew. It was all slipping into history, best forgotten.

'How did you find out?'

'I went to see Netty. She's very ill. They just let me in for a few minutes, and I mentioned Tom's accident and she said, "It was all in the newspapers." That's all. Lots of mumbling, but that was the bit that mattered. It didn't even click at the time, either. It was so stupid. It was only today, at lunchtime, that I realized it would have been the *local* papers – I had been thinking of *The Times*, some-how, and wondering how I could go up to London or somewhere and look in the old copies – and then I realized it would be in Meldon papers and in the library if I was lucky. So I went there in the lunch-hour. It's all on microfilm – you read it through a sort of enlarger thing, and of course I knew the date. It only took five minutes to find it, and the librarian put it in the machine, and there it was, the whole story. And then I had to sign a form, and when I put the date – I hadn't realized. Oh, Tim, I thought I would die! It never was coincidence, surely! I was so frightened. I rang your house and I couldn't get through, they said the lines were busy, because the weather's put something out of action or something. So I ran and ran for the bus and just caught it as it was going out of the bus-station, and all the way I was thinking –'

She was shivering again. She had pulled away from

him, and her face looked small and white in spite of the
freckles, all eyes and blue lips. Hot sweet tea, Tim
thought, for shock; she looked vulnerable, which he had
never dreamed earlier could be possible. She was looking
at him in a strange way.

'Oh, Tim – if you had –'

'Shut up, Rebecca,' he said kindly. He put his arm out
and pulled her against him again, comfortingly. 'Come
and fetch my boots with me, and tell me all about it.
What happened. Then we can forget it. Here, hold me
up.'

He wasn't going to tell her that he had felt it all for
himself, without the newspaper. He had known the lake
had to do with Tom. He had sensed its unkindness the
very first day he had set eyes on it. He staggered along on
the skates, still with his arm round Rebecca, back towards
the log where his boots were. Tom wasn't there any
more. He would never come back now, Tim knew. For a
moment he felt relieved, then he felt as if a part of himself
was missing. Tom *was* himself. Had he ever really been a
ghost, or merely his – Tim's – own imagination? Some
things had no answers. Had Rebecca ever seen herself in
Netty? Perhaps he would get around to asking her. His
feeling towards her suddenly were quite changed, holding her against him, stumbling over the hard ground. If
Tom had still been there, he would have laughed at this
revelation. But Tom had gone.

9

Tom got the sack the same evening. He went home and was knocked nearly senseless by his father's rage, deluged by his mother's despair.

'What *happened*? What *happened*?' his mother screeched at him, but he could not begin to say. The story was already out, and it was not his, only a travesty of the facts embroidered by every tongue that passed it on. The village lived by such excitements, real ones being so scarce. Tom had pounced on Netty out of the willows and carried her away to Hanging Wood where but for the providential arrival of Mr. Pettigrew on the scene he would have . . . '*Really*? Tom Inskip!! Would you ever!'

'I didn't! I never!' Tom wept to his mother, but the village women had already told her.

'Little Miss Netty! And Miss May taking you in like that! And your father working for Mr. Pettigrew nearly forty years now and *you* –'

There weren't words enough to accuse, to belabour, to defend, to sort out the truth from the extravagance.

'Tom Inskip! The quiet one! Would you ever have believed –!'

'I didn't! I didn't!'

Mr. Pettigrew had a gash across his eyebrow where he had fallen and they said Tom had attacked him. Tom had bruises all over where his father had attacked him, and they were the truth, but nobody cared about that, only about the stupendous news of what had happened in

Hanging Wood. Tom would not go out, but lay curled on his bed remembering what had really happened with a kind of astonishment, but he could not tell anybody. Into his great torment Miss May arrived, a pillar of strength against which both his mother and father faltered.

'I want to see him,' she said, and Tom came down to find her sitting at the big scrubbed table in her best and most severe black silk, implacable against the stream of his mother's apologies, flinty towards his father's ill grace.

'Tom!' Her eyes flickered when she saw him; he recognized the expression in them and was aware of her compassion although she said nothing else. For the very first time he felt a grain of comfort. He had not realized how he had come to appreciate her indomitable character. Miss May was the rock upon which the whole village laid their troubles, but she had come to him of her own accord. He thought then that she trusted him better than his own parents did, perhaps knew him better, even loved him more. She had nothing, herself.

'Tom, you have nothing to be ashamed of. I have heard what Netty has to say. Now let me hear you. I believe you will speak the truth.'

'It isn't what they say.'

'I don't know what they say.'

Was the Vicarage really such an ivory tower? Tom could hardly speak; it came so hard after his retreat, after the hysteria and the recriminations and the bangings. His mother and father started to say something but May silenced them with a look.

'I want to hear Tom.'

Silence.

'Tom.'

He did not want to say anything, not even to defend himself. He could not tell them the perfection of it, before Mr. Pettigrew came.

'I went with Netty.'

'How do you mean – *went* with?' his mother hissed.

'Walked with her. Ran. I waited for her –'

'She asked you to go, when you were working?' May asked.

'Yes. I shouldn't have but I did. To the wood. That's all.'

'You went into the wood?'

'Yes.'

'Just walking with the dog?'

'Yes.'

'You didn't stop, or sit down?'

'No. We picked primroses, and walked back.'

'You were walking when you met Mr. Pettigrew?'

'Yes.'

'Why did you run away?'

That had been his weakness, Tom knew. Not to stop and have it all shattered by Mr. Pettigrew there and then. To put it off till later, making it all worse.

'I knew Mr. Pettigrew would be angry. He recognized me.'

'Angry because you were supposed to be working?'

'Yes. And with being with Miss Netty.' His voice was almost a whisper.

May said, gently, 'There is no harm in it.'

'He's old enough to know better!' his mother said. 'A working boy like him! I don't know how –'

'He's only flesh and blood,' May said tartly. 'Netty should have known better than to ask him to go. She was very naughty and almost entirely to blame. I shall go and see Mr. Pettigrew, and ask him to give Tom his job back.'

'Oh, Miss May!'

She was like God, taking decisions.

Tom guessed that she would have a difficult job, remembering Mr. Pettigrew's crashing fall and the chase he must have had after Araminta, but by haytime, when there were never enough hands for the work, he was reinstated. Mr. Angus told Tom's father he could start again. Nothing else was said. Tom, having endured in

147

the meantime the unmerciful ragging of his friends, found that nothing much was changed, save in his own experience, his own awareness of having grown that much older, that much wiser. Less trusting. Life was not necessarily very kind. The only thing that did not change was his feeling for Netty, in spite of what she had let him in for. She was the one star in his dull firmament and the fact that she had taken his hand in hers gave him more joy in retrospect than any other single thing that had ever happened to him. He knew better than to expect anything else ever again, and had no feelings of grief on this account. He saw very little of her – and she was away most of the summer – but he was entirely practical about the situation. He could dream, and dreams were harmless enough. The most he ever permitted himself was to try to draw Netty now that his skill was improving, but even this was more of a laugh than a spiritual communication. He burned most of the drawings, but kept the only one which had a remote likeness to her in a tin box up the chimney. His father did not like his drawing. He was too busy to go for lessons all through the harvest, but afterwards Miss May asked him to come again. He went, but he hardly ever saw Netty.

'Tom!'

Tom turned round from the haystack where he and Arnold were chopping out hay for the next feed.

'I've got a job for you, lad. Get down here quick sharp. Young Arnold can finish that on 'is own.'

Tom groaned to himself, doubting whether the job was an improvement on hay-chopping. Surprisingly, it was.

'This parcel's come for Mr. Pettigrew. It's seeds, an' they've sent it up the farm by mistake. I know 'e's waiting for these, for 'is green'ouse, so you cut along up there and give 'em to Mr. Ford the gardener. Nobody else is going

148

that way today. Mr. Pettigrew'll be out huntin', but 'e'll be pleased if they're there when 'e gets 'ome.'

Tom shoved the small parcel in his jacket pocket and set off without a word. It was two miles to Curlews from the farm, and two miles back, with the faint possibility of a cup of tea from the kitchen if he was lucky, not to mention the earning of a penny or two if he happened to be around to hold a gate where hounds were drawing. The prospect was infinitely more rewarding than hay-chopping.

Tim, possibly, wouldn't have thought so. It was cold after a long period of frost, but raw rather than crisp, with all the bare branches dripping overhead, and the lane deep with half-frozen mud. A thin sleet was falling. Tom could feel the dampness in his socks and across his shoulders through the threadbare jacket. He pulled his cap well down and set off at a calculated pace, not fast enough to get an easy job over too soon, not so slow that he would get a clout for being too long. He didn't feel very marvellous, for some reason – possibly something to do with sitting too long yesterday under the church wall drawing Curlews. The sun had shone for an hour, and he had hidden himself away from the graveyard visitors in a sheltered spot and drawn the bleak sunlit view of the old house on the ridge with the winter trees sharp against a dull sky. It had gone well and he had forgotten how cold it was until he had stood up and the wind had found him over the wall, pushing itself right through the shiny serge of his Sunday suit as if the suit were a mere farm sack. He had scurried back through the churchyard. A brief, flaming sunset was scorching the horizon, inked over by a mesh of old elms and black hedgerow and circling rooks; Miss May was coming back from the Sunday-school, pinched about the face with cold, and Tom had been unable to avoid her. She had looked at his drawing, and her face had unparched with pleasure at his efforts.

'*Very* good, Tom! A lovely feeling of distance . . .'

She had always been on at him to draw in his mythical spare time; she hadn't commented on the fact that he had cut church to draw. She couldn't have it all ways. Tom had gone on home with her approbation lingering in his ears, warmed by her praise. Miss May had proved a staunch friend to him over the past year, perhaps one of the reasons he still persevered with the drawing, because he did not want to disappoint her.

To get to Curlews he took a short cut through the churchyard, down through the empty corner under the elms and over the wall where he had been drawing the day before. He pulled out a dead stick and bashed at the stiff, frosty stalks of brown bracken to try to warm himself; he had a strange feeling that he was not alone, as if there was someone else going down the track towards the lake. He turned round once or twice to see, and stopped and listened, but decided it was the hallucinations of an empty stomach, his stomach feeling empty more often than full. He was small for his age ('All skin and bone,' his grandma said – 'A lean dog for a hard road,' said his father), but lately had been growing out of his clothes, to his own satisfaction, if not his mother's. Turning to look behind now, and taking a long step forward at the same time, he heard the now familiar splitting noise of yet another defeated seam. It was followed almost immediately by a sound that he knew wasn't a hallucination at all: the distant echo from the fields behind him of Mr. Pettigrew's hunting-horn. He stopped to marshall his wits, not wanting to miss anything. He knew where hounds had met and he knew the ways of the foxes; if he could hear the horn again, or the music of the pack, he might be able to guess where they were likely to appear. Or possibly Mr. Pettigrew might bring them down to draw his own home covert.

He went on down the hill, but slowly, waiting. The lake lay below, frozen, but with water shining over the ice. A woodpecker was drilling somewhere, and a spring ran down through the peat with a hollow gurgling noise, nurturing the brightness of a patch of moss and hart's tongues. Tom, seeing, wondered if he could smell the suggestion of summer; it never failed to excite, the eternal promise, the only one that never disappointed. He stopped again. Silence. Drops of water falling. His own breath. Then, suddenly, quite close, a rustling in the bracken.

Tom kept still.

The vixen came past almost within touching distance, sneaking low to the ground over the moss, then bounding down through the bracken with a long easy stride. She was not pushed, or even anxious, intent on her cunning. Tom saw it, and laughed. He lost sight of her, but knew where to look, down on the edge of the lake. She came, and paused, then trotted cautiously out over the ice.

'Clever little beggar.'

Tom went more slowly, spinning it out. If he saw where she went away on the other side, and told the huntsman, he would very likely get something for his trouble, and certainly please Mr. Pettigrew. Pleasing Mr. Pettigrew was not to be sneezed at, to balance out the times he was far more likely to displease him; it mattered, unfortunately, to please Mr. Pettigrew. On the other hand, Tom's heart was with the vixen. He could hear hounds now, crashing and yelping through the woods behind the Vicarage. He stopped to wait. Mermaid was in the pack now, and if the field ever caught up with them Netty would be there on the pony she had borrowed from Pettigrew, urging her own particular darling on without any regard at all for etiquette. Tom realized he might be in luck all ways. He did not see what was going to happen until it was too late to prevent it.

Hounds streamed over the churchyard wall and down the hill behind him. He stayed still and they went past, muddy and intent, loping and leaping down the tawny hill-side like a part of it come to life, an avalanche of sudden movement. Their speed surprised Tom. He guessed they had a view but, having taken his eyes off the vixen he could not see her again, although he thought that by now she was on the other side of the lake.

The leading hound reached the waterside and checked, but a pair behind jumped out on to the ice and ran on strongly. As the pack converged on the lakeside, some went out on the ice after the two leaders and others hung back, casting about hesitantly. Tom frowned, anxious suddenly for the impetuous ones, but there was no huntsman in sight yet to call them off. The older hounds sensed the danger, but the younger ones were too eager to be put off. Tom saw another couple go skating away, running and sliding and throwing their tongues in an ecstasy of excitement, straight towards the centre of the lake.

'Oh, God!' Tom could see it all happening now. He ran down through the bracken, shouting at them to come back, trying to remember out of all the peculiar calls he had heard the huntsman use which was the one of reprimand, to return. The thaw was too far gone to bear the hounds' weight; only the light passing of the clever vixen could use it. The leading pair of hounds were already through, and the next pair sliding to a halt with sudden whimpers of fear, but too late. By the time Tom got to the lakeside there was a spreading, shaking hole of black water with ten hounds howling and threshing about, trying to return. But they were well out from the bank, about sixty feet, and there was nothing he could do about it.

But by now, much to Tom's relief, the huntsman was in sight at the top of the ridge, jumping out of the Vicarage wood, the rest of the field bundling up behind him for the thinnest place in the hedge. He had a clear picture of what was going on as he galloped down the hill, and pulled up beside Tom with a stream of lurid language directed at the world in general.

'Couldn't you have stopped them, boy?' he shouted. 'Here, hold my horse! God's truth, our luck this morning –! Picture! Up, girl! Here, girl! Diamond! Mermaid!'

Tom was flung a bundle of sweaty reins and found himself in charge of a wheeling, snorting, ill-tempered mare in a frenzy to go on galloping. Simultaneously he heard the call, 'Mermaid!' and his spirits plunged. Up to now the incident was really nothing to do with him at all. Now he was involved. Harry the huntsman, a spit-fire old devil who cared for nobody, not even Mr. Pettigrew himself, was stamping out on to the ice cracking his whip and bawling into the sleety wind and behind him down the hill a stream of riders and steaming horses were converging on the little drama, crashing through the brambles, sliding and swearing to a confused halt, shouting advice before they were at a standstill.

'Watch it, Harry! Mind you don't go!'

'Get some branches!'

'Someone go and fetch a rope from Curlews.'

Mr. Pettigrew was there, striding forward to take command. The wiser hounds plunged up and down the bank, whimpering and crying, aware that something had gone wrong. Tom managed to calm Harry's mare so that he had a chance to take stock. The field numbered about twenty, and the more forceful characters among them were already dismounted and out on the ice after Harry; the ladies in their silk hats and veils were trying to hold the men's horses and keep their composure at the same time, as well as get a view of what was going on.

'Do be careful!' they cried.

'Mind out, lad. Let's come through!' Pettigrew and another farmer backed against Tom, dragging a fallen branch after them. Tom moved the mare round and got out of the way.

'Give 'em something to get a hold on!'

'Shove it out in front of you, John! Go steady!'

'Aye, it's breaking everywhere. Be careful!'

The men on the ice were forced to retreat only about a quarter of the way out to the hounds, the ice bending in a peculiarly horrible fashion so that the water came surging in as if it had a tide under it. Two large cracks sprang up, grinding, ominous, and the men slid back, scared. Pettigrew was angry.

'Push these branches out! We can't leave them there to drown, all our best bitches! Call them out, Harry! Give them heart!'

'The cold's getting 'em.'

'Come up, Mermaid! Stately, Rivulet! Come up, girls! Try, Diamond!'

The hounds, swimming valiantly, kept striking at the edge of the ice, but could get no grip and each time fell back. Or else the ice gave, the hole spreading, the black water fingering out, spurting up through the cracks. Tom could sense their desperation, the tiring, thrusting, scrabbling paws finding no substance, each time dropping back more wearily.

'Come on, man! Hurry!'

'They can't keep that up for long!'

'Mermaid! Mermaid!'

Netty was on the bank, screaming at her own dear hound. Tom saw her, holding up her habit, jump out on to the ice.

'Come back, m'dear!'

Harry swore at her, catching her arm, but she ran out. Pettigrew skated out after her, shoving the big branch ahead of him.

'Come here, you little fool! Come back! We'll get her if you keep your head!'

'Mermaid! *Mermaid*! Try!'

One of the men pulled her back, sobbing. There was mud all over her habit and her tears, copious and un-

154

ashamed, washed the mud on her face. Tom felt himself quiver.

The branches were cautiously edged out across the ice as far as the men were able to take them.

'You're too heavy, Mr. Pettigrew!' Harry called. 'Get someone lighter to go a little farther! Be careful, sir!'

'Let me go!' Netty cried, leaping forward. 'Let me! I'm the lightest!'

'No, girl, use sense! This isn't for the ladies!' Harry straightened up and glanced round at the circle of spectators. His eyes found his own mare, and flickered to Tom.

'You, lad. How about you?'

'He's light enough.' Pettigrew, returning, beckoned him out with an employer's finger.

'Oh, Tom!' Netty rounded on him like a consuming flame, her eyes alight with eager tears. 'Mermaid *knows* you – do fetch her, Tom! *Please*, Tom! Oh, please, Tom, for me!'

Tom was cornered and knew it. Someone took the mare's reins out of his hands. He didn't want to go at all. He wasn't brave. Pettigrew wouldn't force him, he knew, but Netty –

'Tom, *please*!'

Soft golden freckles shining with tears, her face pleading, so close he could see his own reflection in her fantastic navy-blue eyes . . . he felt his insides turn to water, whether for fear or for love he was never to know. It wasn't much, after all, to push a branch a bit farther out. He went forward and over the ice with Pettigrew, where it was thick, and heard Netty behind him shouting, clear and gleeful, 'Mermaid! Mermaid, Tom is coming to get you! Hold on!' The ice was furry on top with thaw, ugly and yellow and flawed. Tom felt his feet sliding, and heard the creaking under Pettigrew. The water was all through his thin boot soles and into the warm fug of his socks. The sleet bit at his face and the hounds cried to him, struggling in the dark, threshing pool.

'Push the big one a bit farther – spread the weight. Hold on to it! Manley has gone to get a rope, he won't be long – a ladder . . . then we'll do it. But if they have something to support them – they won't last much longer. The cold'll have them.'

Between them they pushed and struggled with the big branch. Ahead of it, lying on the ice, was a long, lighter sapling. Tom got to the front of the heavy branch and reached out for the sapling to give it as hearty a shrug as he had strength for – he wasn't liking it very much and decided that that was as far as his courage would take him. He had never pretended to great courage. He had run away from Pettigrew at the last crisis in his life. But now Pettigrew was saying, 'Good lad. That's it!' and he could hear the joy in Netty's voice behind him, 'Tom, well done, Tom!'

The water was over his ankles, the ice sinking beneath him. 'Oh, God,' he thought, 'let me get back!' He shoved at the wretched sapling with all his strength, moving it sluggishly forward, and at the same time felt the ice lurch beneath him. It didn't so much crack as merely disappear. It went away from him, his feet with it, and he was on his back and sliding, the thick granules of old ice grating under his scrabbling hands until the water floated them, and took him at the same time in an embrace so cold that his senses seemed to explode with the shock. He hadn't meant to be a hero! The searing, crushing, drowning dark and the roaring of the black water inside his very head, filling his mouth and his ears and his nose and his eyes – God, he had no breath at all! He was the ice, too, spinning round in the black pool. He threshed out, meeting ice and yelping, panicking hound. He was fighting, screaming, but no screams could survive the cold to issue forth on the freezing air, merely gasps and chokings and all the other agonized noises to find air; he heard them in his own head, splitting his skull. The panic drove him, fighting, but his lungs would not try, splintered with pain. A flailing hand caught something hard, clutched, scrabbled, caught. There was the sky suddenly, grey with flakes of snow darker instead of light, driving soft and dark and furry over the sky, grey and melting into the black water. He caught his own sapling and crooked his elbow round it, but still the breath couldn't get to him, nor the screams escape. The sky grew darker.

'Oh, my God!'
   'Who went for a ladder? A rope? Is he –'
   'Hurry! Hurry! There's a ladder at –'
   'Go then! Manley must have got lost!'
   'Oh, God, hurry –'
   'Try this branch!'
   'Don't risk anybody else.'
The horses, steaming, stamped with boredom, snatching at reins. The snow, in large wet flakes, touched them and vanished; the ladies, holding them, wept. Netty, standing on the ice, the hem of her habit awash, screamed, 'Tom! Tom! Hold on! *Please*! Tom! Mermaid! Oh, Mermaid!'
   'What a day! What a day!'
The men, stamping up and down, kept watching for the man with the ladder, watching Tom and the hounds, cursing and muttering. They could get no farther than the big branch without the ice making its gruesome dipping and creaking, and Tom then was still out of reach, hanging with one arm over the sapling, and one laid out, claw-fingered, on the one piece of ice that had not so far cracked under his weight. He made no sound, and his head was turned away, and no one knew how he looked in his extremity; they could only see the desperate hand holding. The hounds had kept plunging at him, knocking him farther away into the breaking ice; he had gone under several times, but now the hounds were too

157

exhausted to bother him. Three had already disappeared and two more were floating without any movement.

'Damn that vixen! Damn her!' Harry wept, or else his eyes were watering with cold.

'Ah, we might be lucky!' Pettigrew growled. 'He's not given in yet!'

'That shrimp – he's half-starved and has had congestion of the lungs twice this winter,' said the doctor. 'This'll finish him.'

'They're tough, these brats –'

'Have to be, the way you work 'em, Pettigrew,' said the doctor.

'Here's your ladder coming! Now we'll get 'im!'

Reinforcements from the village were appearing at the top of the ridge, armed with ladders, hurdles and ropes. They came plunging down the slope, curious and excited, and the horses were reined out of the way to let them through. The churned bank was cleared and the hurdles and the ladders slipped out over the ice, the boys who took them trailing safety ropes behind them. The spectators closed in again, silent now, their faces tight and cold.

'It's too long –'

'They'll get him! Ah, watch it, Arthur, lad!'

'That ice'll all go in a minute.'

Stumbling down the hill, an umbrella clutched in one hand, her skirts in the other, May Bellinger arrived among the group unnoticed. She pushed her way to the ice, shouldering her way through, and pulled the weeping Netty round to face her.

'Is is true what they say? It's Tom –'

'Tom and Mermaid,' Netty sobbed.

'Oh, my dear!' May seemed to shrink, to wither, the snow touching her, its whiteness showing the ivory pallor of her face. Beside her Netty was bright with weeping, hot and gold and dishevelled with the excitement of her grief.

'Tom! I told him –! I asked him!'

'My darling.'

May did not move, watching. There was a web of hurdles spread round the hole, and the ice was swaying and groaning. Nobody could see quite what was happening for the men who were splayed out, reaching, muttering. The ropes trailed back to the bank. The ice muttered and cracked. Someone let out a yelp of alarm; the water in the hole rushed forward and retreated . . . a scurry and legs kicking –

'*Hold* him!'

'I've got you! Quick!'

'No – mind! Steady, I've got him. Pull – pull me –'

'Oh, God! Wait a bit. I can't –'

'Hurry, I can't hold him much longer!'

'Pull! Pull!'

The ropes tightened on the hurdles, strained. The ice started to crack, starring like a splintered mirror with black fountains pressing up here and there, spurting and subsiding. The men farthest out were wriggling frantically and the ice beneath them was sagging, letting up waves of the black water, the hole opening out. The hurdles were dragged back and Tom's body broke the ice again and again, lifted and dragged and almost let go again, the man holding it almost going too. The water beneath them was, by legend, fifty feet deep and they knew it, the panic breaking in them at each setback, with flurries and curses and sobs.

'Now *pull*!'

'Oh, God, I can't!'

'Now!'

Tom's body came with a rush, spread-eagled on the hurdle. His hands fell on the ice, still clutching, the fingers to the sky. The men wriggled backwards, grotesquely spread out, groaning at the sodden dead weight they had to drag inch by inch. The men on the bank went out to meet them, too impetuous – the ice cracked again

159

and they scurried back. Pettigrew went out alone and when the men were able to stand up he picked Tom off the hurdle and carried him to the shore in his arms. They all came to the bank together, and the crowd fell back.

Tom saw Netty. He had this sensation of her warming him again, as if she were a fire, so close that the sheaf of her red-gold hair was touching his face. Miss May was there too, but not so close. There was an expression on her face that reminded him of something he had seen before. He tried to think what it was, but Netty kept saying something; he could see her lips moving. He wanted to ask her what she wanted, but there seemed to be no provision in his body for talking. Not for anything. It was a most curious sensation. Miss May's face – yes, he remembered. It was the evening on the lawn when her cat had died. Ferdy. How extraordinary! Why should she be looking like that now? There was nothing wrong. Nothing at all. But he couldn't say anything, although his lips framed the word, 'Ferdy'.

'*What* did he say?'

'He said Ferdy,' Netty said.

'Ferdy?' May, holding Netty through her tempest of noisy grief, did not understand how Tom could have meant Ferdy, although it had such meaning for her.

'It was "Netty", I should think,' she whispered.

'It's finished,' the doctor said, straightening up. 'We'd better carry him up to Curlews on a hurdle, and take him home in a cart.

May, holding Netty, thinking that she had never loved anyone in all her life save her mother, now knew better. She was silent. The thaw had come but it was still very cold. She saw the beginnings of a hard green catkin growing on a hazel twig above the churned mud of the bank. It was the sort of thing she would have broken off to take home for Tom to draw that evening. But Tom wouldn't draw anything else again.

She said quietly to Netty, 'I'll take you home.'

She took Netty's hand and led her away. The people stood back for her, respectfully silent. When she had gone they pressed forward again, not wanting to miss anything, and saw the bedraggled body laid back on the hurdle, the eyelids pressed down, the arms gathered tidily. The men lifted it, and the horses started to move away; Harry called the remains of his pack, Pettigrew cursed.

In the woods on the other side of the lake the vixen lay by her earth, licking the mud off her paws.

10

Tim sat among all the upheaval of the house-removing, feeling that very little of it concerned him at all. The only thing he had a pang for was the crooked little room where he had slept. He wished it well with its new owners. He had already moved out to George's, where he slept on a sagging divan in a room full of home-made jam and stored apples. For board and keep George had docked him two pounds out of the five, so he now existed on the princely sum of three pounds a week. His father, on hearing of the deal, offered to send him to art school.

'You can live at home, come and go as you please. You haven't even had the manners to come and inspect your new home yet. Your mother has been expecting you every week-end.'

The new home was in Esher, in Surrey. Tim could guess very well what it was like and didn't want to know. He declined his father's offer. It had come too late. Having cut his teeth on manual labour and got through the nastiest part of the year, he now positively enjoyed banging out horseshoes and yarning in the yard under the walnut tree with Josh and Len from the farm, and Biddy from the riding-school and Arthur with the point-to-point horses. George went racing every Saturday and Wednesday and Tim had two full days off to paint. George didn't believe in overwork.

'What's the good of being your own boss if you can't take a day off when you like?' It had occurred to Tim that

George was a completely happy man, which his father was not.

'You're making a dreadful mistake,' his mother had said over and over again. Everybody thought this, except Rebecca. Tim wasn't sure. He thought it might prove so in the end, if he was unlucky; on the other hand the feeling of freedom which he had first enjoyed had never left him. He had met a lot of new people who, if not smart, were genuine and he thought he preferred their outlook to that of his parents' acquaintances. Of his own friends at school the ones he most cared about thought what he had done was 'great', but he felt that they thought it great in a freakish sense; he did not feel that any of them intended to emulate him.

'How will you ever better yourself?' his mother asked. 'What happens when you want to marry and buy a house and have four children? On three pounds a week?'

'Two children,' said Tim automatically. His expensive education, among other things, had grounded him thoroughly in the problems his own generation had got to face. They were no less, by his becoming a blacksmith.

'It's a more useful job than my father's,' he said.

His mother nearly exploded.

'It's not just horses' feet. It's all sorts of things.' His mother wouldn't listen, but he could have enlarged happily on the making of hinges, firebacks, bolts, machinery parts, towing bars and mock-Tudor light-brackets. He was good at it and knew it. He had always enjoyed the mechanics and the satisfactions of that type of craftsmanship, half mental, half physical; he could lose all track of time following a job through.

'Look at your hands!'

Tim shrugged.

'I'm all right, can't you see?' Couldn't she get interested in something else, instead of him?

'Your father's not sending you any money, you know that?'

'Yes, I know.'

It was as good as the Meldon council-house now; he had risen to the height of poverty and deprivation that Rebecca had so desired. He went to the Vicarage whenever he had time, and Rebecca made him baked beans on toast and he helped her with her pollution studies. He couldn't afford to take her out.

His mother went to interfere with the removing men, then came back and said, 'This letter is for you. I had forgotten all about it. I found it here on the mat when I came last Friday.'

Tim took it. The postmark was Denbigh. He had written to an address in Denbigh last February at Rebecca's urgent instigation, and had forgotten all about it. He opened it curiously, not knowing what to expect, not wanting any problems raised. Tom's ghost was laid; he did not want it disturbed. The writing was frail and wobbly, but beautifully formed.

'Dear Tim. You wrote to me some weeks ago at the time of my cousin Netty's death, inquiring about the boy Tom Inskip whose story you were interested in. I am afraid I am too ancient now to travel away from home, otherwise I would have come to poor Netty's funeral and would have enjoyed meeting you and your friend Rebecca. However, I will do my best to answer your questions in this letter.

'Yes, I still remember Tom, although it is so many years now since he died. The accident was very tragic, and Netty blamed herself for it afterwards. It was a great shock to us all, but Netty was changed by it. She seemed to grow up very quickly afterwards and became far more serious and responsible. When the war broke out she became a V.A.D. and went to France, as indeed I did myself on the death of my father. In many ways the war was a great liberation for us women, although one cannot

164

say the same for the men, as those that survived in many cases came back to worse conditions than they had suffered before. I often thought of this particularly in respect of Tom. His was such a sweet nature that if he had lived I think perhaps he would have suffered more in many ways than he did by dying in the way God chose for him. His life though short was very happy, for he demanded very little and accepted what he had with a perfect spiritual grace. This I do not expect you as a young person to understand, and whether in fact it is a good thing or not I would not like to say. I am only stating what I know was true. His drawing was very remarkable in a village boy, and whether, if he had lived, he would have made anything of it I cannot say. As for Netty and myself, our ways parted and we saw little of each other in later life. She went to India after the war, and travelled all over the world. Although she always had many friends, she never married, which was surprising, and I do not know the reason for it. I married in 1920 and was fortunate enough to be blessed with a dear husband and three fine children, and now two grandchildren as well. I suffer from arthritis and cannot get about now, but I have my family around me and God's blessings for which I am eternally grateful.

Yours affectionately,
May Parsons.

P.S. I think Tom was always more than a little in love with Netty, but nobody loved Tom more dearly than myself.

M.P.'

Tim read this letter three times. Rebecca had got the name and address of Netty's next-of-kin from the hospital when Netty had died, and had persuaded him to write a letter to her after a decent interval had elapsed. Their only clue had been the Christian name May. She had been described as a cousin. 'It must be the same one, May

Bellinger,' Rebecca had insisted. 'The name on the piano music – and I thought she was Netty's sister. It must be the Miss May who taught Tom drawing!' Tim, reluctantly, had written, describing the drawings they had found, and the story they had uncovered in the old newspaper. He didn't say a word about knowing Tom Inskip any more intimately than through the name on a gravestone. He had not described just how well he did know Tom Inskip, the way he looked and the way he talked and teased and dressed and knew about things. He had then forgotten all about it, although Rebecca inquired from time to time. And now –

'What is it?' his mother asked.

'Nothing.'

It was finished. May would shortly follow Netty, and the era which had ended so prematurely for Tom would be rounded off in its due season, and sink into mere memories, books, and hear-say. No one else would ever recall Tom Inskip after himself; even the inscription on the gravestone would not be deciphered for more than another year or two. He folded the letter up and put it in his pocket. He would show it to Rebecca – she could keep it if she liked.

Strangely, although he had not intended to think about it any more, there was one sentence in May's letter that kept coming back to him. 'His life though short was very happy, for he demanded very little and accepted what he had with a perfect spiritual grace.' The phrasing was quaint, even corny, a sort of text-for-today flavour about it, yet it stayed with Tim with uncanny insistence. It was relevant, in many ways. 'He demanded very little' – bed, board, and three pounds a week – 'and accepted what he had' – bed, board, and three pounds a week – 'with perfect spiritual grace.' Perfect spiritual grace presumably meant a contented frame of mind. Did he accept it with perfect spiritual grace? If he didn't make up his mind now he wouldn't have the chance again. He discussed it with

Rebecca, and it came to be called between them by its initials, P.S.G.

'What *do* you want then, if you haven't got it now?' Rebecca asked him somewhat impatiently.

'A big, fast car,' Tim said.

'Then do what your mummy and daddy want, and daddy will buy you one.'

Tim pondered. 'I want P.S.G. as well, and I won't get it that way.'

'No. Well, decide.'

'I have decided really, you know that.'

Rebecca smiled one of her rare, redeeming smiles. She could not hide her missionary antecedents at such moments, which made Tim laugh.

Rebecca said, 'You don't have to stay George's minion on three pounds a week for ever. You'll work up to a car, if not the sort your father's got. George has got a car.'

'If I'm lucky,' Tim said slowly, having given the matter a lot of thought during the past few weeks, 'I might build up a business of my own, more the domestic side of it than the horses, because I'm not really a horsy person – I recognize my limitations. Or even the church side – there's quite a demand for really good church stuff which has to be designed as well as made – altar railings, crucifixes, candle-holders, all that sort of thing. There are lots of possibilities. And evening classes and courses for that sort of design – other people to learn from when I'm ready. It needn't be just a dead-end thing, which my parents think it is. If I'm good enough, that is.'

He considered. 'There have to be openings, ambitions, even in this. Otherwise it is back to Tom again. There was nothing for him. And I don't think Tom – some of them, perhaps, but not Tom – was so dumb that he would have been perfectly happy labouring for Mr. Pettigrew until he died of old age. I think his P.S.G. would have worn thin. I don't know why I keep coming back to Tom. He's gone now.'

'I think he brought you to life,' Rebecca said.

Tim looked at her to see if she was smiling. She wasn't. Sometimes she embarrassed him with the strange, earnest things she said; sometimes he wondered if she wasn't right more often than he gave her credit for. He would miss her now, very much, he realized, if they were parted.

'Perhaps.'

After all, who would ever know exactly what Tom's role in life had been, let alone in death?

More Beaver Books

On the following pages you will find some other exciting Beaver Books to look out for in your local bookshop

BEAVER BOOKS FOR OLDER READERS

There are loads of exciting books for older readers in Beaver.
They are available in bookshops or they can be ordered directly
from us. Just complete the form below and send the right
amount of money and the books will be sent to you at home.

☐	THE RUNAWAYS	Ruth Thomas	£1.99
☐	COMPANIONS ON THE ROAD	Tanith Lee	£1.99
☐	THE GOOSEBERRY	Joan Lingard	£1.95
☐	IN THE GRIP OF WINTER	Colin Dann	£2.50
☐	THE TEMPEST TWINS Books 1 – 6	John Harvey	£1.99
☐	YOUR FRIEND, REBECCA	Linda Hoy	£1.99
☐	THE TIME OF THE GHOST	Diana Wynne Jones	£1.95
☐	WATER LANE	Tom Aitken	£1.95
☐	ALANNA	Tamora Pierce	£2.50
☐	REDWALL	Brian Jacques	£2.95
☐	BUT JASPER CAME INSTEAD	Christine Nostlinger	£1.95
☐	A BOTTLED CHERRY ANGEL	Jean Ure	£1.99
☐	A HAWK IN SILVER	Mary Gentle	£1.99
☐	WHITE FANG	Jack London	£1.95
☐	FANGS OF THE WEREWOLF	John Halkin	£1.95

If you would like to order books, please send this form, and the money
due to:
ARROW BOOKS, BOOKSERVICE BY POST, PO BOX 29,
DOUGLAS, ISLE OF MAN, BRITISH ISLES. Please enclose a
cheque or postal order made out to Arrow Books Ltd for the amount
due including 22p per book for postage and packing both for orders
within the UK and for overseas orders.

NAME ....

ADDRESS ....

....

Please print clearly.

Whilst every effort is made to keep prices low it is sometimes necessary
to increase cover prices at short notice. Arrow Books reserve the right to
show new retail prices on covers which may differ from those
previously advertised in the text or elsewhere.

JOAN LINGARD

If you enjoyed this book, perhaps you ought to try some of our Joan Lingard titles. They are available in bookshops or they can be ordered directly from us. Just complete the form below and enclose the right amount of money and the book will be sent to you at home.

If you would like to order books, please send this form, and the money due to:
ARROW BOOKS, BOOKSERVICE BY POST, PO BOX 29, DOUGLAS, ISLE OF MAN, BRITISH ISLES. Please enclose a cheque or postal order made out to Arrow Books Ltd for the amount due including 22p per book for postage and packing both for orders within the UK and for overseas orders.

NAME ....

ADDRESS ....

....

Please print clearly.

Whilst every effort is made to keep prices low it is sometimes necessary to increase cover prices at short notice. Arrow Books reserve the right to show new retail prices on covers which may differ from those previously advertised in the text or elsewhere.

BEAVER BESTSELLERS

You'll find books for everyone to enjoy from Beaver's bestselling range—there are hilarious joke books, gripping reads, wonderful stories, exciting poems and fun activity books. They are available in bookshops or they can be ordered directly from us. Just complete the form below and send the right amount of money and the books will be sent to you at home.

☐ THE ADVENTURES OF KING ROLLO	David McKee	£2.50
☐ MR PINK-WHISTLE STORIES	Enid Blyton	£1.95
☐ FOLK OF THE FARAWAY TREE	Enid Blyton	£1.99
☐ REDWALL	Brian Jacques	£2.95
☐ STRANGERS IN THE HOUSE	Joan Lingard	£1.95
☐ THE RAM OF SWEETRIVER	Colin Dann	£2.50
☐ BAD BOYES	Jim and Duncan Eldridge	£1.95
☐ ANIMAL VERSE	Raymond Wilson	£1.99
☐ A JUMBLE OF JUNGLY JOKES	John Hegarty	£1.50
☐ THE RETURN OF THE ELEPHANT JOKE BOOK	Katie Wales	£1.50
☐ THE REVENGE OF THE BRAIN SHARPENERS	Philip Curtis	£1.50
☐ THE RUNAWAYS	Ruth Thomas	£1.99
☐ EAST OF MIDNIGHT	Tanith Lee	£1.99
☐ THE BARLEY SUGAR GHOST	Hazel Townson	£1.50
☐ CRAZY COOKING	Juliet Bawden	£2.25

If you would like to order books, please send this form, and the money due to:
ARROW BOOKS, BOOKSERVICE BY POST, PO BOX 29, DOUGLAS, ISLE OF MAN, BRITISH ISLES. Please enclose a cheque or postal order made out to Arrow Books Ltd for the amount due including 22p per book for postage and packing both for orders within the UK and for overseas orders.

NAME ....

ADDRESS ....

....

Please print clearly.

Whilst every effort is made to keep prices low it is sometimes necessary to increase cover prices at short notice. Arrow Books reserve the right to show new retail prices on covers which may differ from those previously advertised in the text or elsewhere.